FOLLOWED

LONDON CRIME THRILLER SERIES
BOOK 1

CARA ALEXANDER

Copyright © 2020 by Cara Alexander

All rights reserved.

No part of this book may be reproduced in any form or by any electronic or mechanical means, including information storage and retrieval systems, without written permission from the author, except for the use of brief quotations in a book review.

This story is a work of fiction. All names, characters, organisations or places, events and incidents are products of the author's imagination or are used fictitiously.

EXCLUSIVE OFFER!

Be the first to get news about my upcoming books. Receive a free copy of the prequel to the London Crime Thriller Series PLUS you can join my review team and read my books before they're published.
All this and more - Join today for free at www.caraaalexander.com

I look forward to seeing you on the inside.

———

Never miss a new release.
No spam, ever, guaranteed. You can unsubscribe at any time.

ALSO BY CARA ALEXANDER

The Killing

Panic

Payback

Pure Evil

Fallout

Fatal Intent

Nemesis

In Too Deep

1

LONDON

Paddington Station
Early September

THE BUS SWAYS around Marble Arch, then turns left onto Edgware Road. I glance at my phone. My train leaves in twelve minutes. If this bus doesn't get a move on, I'll never make it.

Suddenly the bus gathers speed and turns from Edgware Road into Praed Street. Ten minutes later, it squeals to a halt outside Paddington Tube Station.

Leaping off the bus, I sprint across the street. A cyclist curses. I ignore him and run down the small side street into London Paddington train station, and stand searching for the overhead information board.

Someone nudges me.

I turn and look to see who it is.

It's a guy of about eighteen and he's pointing straight ahead of me. 'It's over there, the board's over there!'

'Thanks!'

He gives me a grin, then turns and runs to catch his train.

I stand scanning the board. London to Oxford leaves in two minutes, but the station's heaving with people. Can I make it?

Maneuvering my way through the crowded station, I run as fast as I can to the platform, swipe my ticket over the automatic barrier, and jump on the train.

Flopping down on one of the pale blue seats I sigh with relief glad I made it.

The whistle blows, doors close, and the train clanks and groans its way out of Paddington station.

With my face pressed against the window, I gaze at the passing warehouses and rows of old London terraced houses and think of the terrible interview I just had. What a waste of time that was. They didn't want a political reporter all they wanted was someone to dish the dirt on what was happening at Westminster.

'Mind if I sit here?'

Opening my eyes, I see a scruffy-looking guy peering into my face, then he points to the seat beside me.

I turn and look around. There's a man at the far end of the carriage reading his newspaper, otherwise the carriage is empty.

I gesture to the rows of empty seats. 'There are lots of seats over there.'

He just ignores me, plonks himself down, and mutters, 'No, I'd rather sit here.'

Then, stretching out his long thin legs, he gives me a sly sideway look. I can feel my cheeks burning. His voice is weird, quite high pitched. He has watery blue eyes, a droopy looking brown moustache and limp, greasy brown hair.

What a shit day and now I have this idiot to deal with. If

I was on the Tube, I could understand it. People crammed together like sardines, but this train is empty.

He sits staring at me with a horrible sneer on his face. It's as if he's challenging me to say something. I feel like punching him in the face, but I don't.

Without looking at him, I get up and walk through the train. I'll find another seat with people nearby.

An hour later, the train pulls into Oxford. This is where I get off.

I'm just about to leave the station when I think of my friend Helen. Her parents died in a car accident a year ago and she hasn't been back to their house since it happened. She asked if I could check on it for her. It's only a short train ride from Mum's so now might be a good time to do it.

Instead of leaving the station at Oxford, I change platforms and wait for the train to Evesly, where her house is. It's a lovely day — it will only take twenty minutes by train — I'll have enough time to check the house, then collect my son Jamie from school.

A few minutes later, the train arrives, but unlike the train from London, this one is quite busy. Heaving a sigh of relief, I enter the train — no more empty carriages for me today.

Fields of corn and honey coloured Cotswold stone houses flash by the train's window reminding me of how lovely it is. This is where I met Helen. The house I lived in was just around the corner from hers. After school, we'd often take the shortcut and walk through the golden fields of corn to where we lived. It was at the back of the station. I wonder if it's still there.

I sigh and settle down. I'll take a quick peek at Helen's home, make sure everything's alright, and then collect Jamie from school.

. . .

Twenty minutes later, I'm walking out of Evesly station and peering around to see if anything's changed, but nothing has. Everything still looks more or less the same as when I lived here. It's one of those typical sleepy Cotswold villages where everyone knows each other. When I lived here, my parents had jobs at a college in Oxford, then Dad's mum got sick and we had to return to Athens.

I sling my jacket over my shoulder and stroll around to the rear of the station. Although it's a bit overgrown the path's still here, and on a day like today, who wants to take the bus when it's only a ten-minute walk through the field.

As I stroll along the overgrown pathway, I inhale the familiar scent of wildflowers and corn. It's early September, so a lovely time to be in the country, especially on such a warm sunny day. The blackberry bushes are heavy with fruit. I stop and pick one — they still taste good. Then I freeze — it sounded like a twig or something breaking behind me. I stop and listen, but all I can hear is the sound of birds tweeting int he air and the rustle of corn in the breeze.

Am I imagining it?

I turn to look, but nobody's there.

Walking a little faster, I can soon see the top of Helen's house poking out from the row of houses where she lives. Not far to go, just a few minutes and I'll be there.

The sound of a twig snapping again makes me stop — I'm not imagining it.

Then, to my horror, someone laughs.

I swing round, but before I can see who it is, something's thrown over my head — I try pulling it off, but it's too tight, so I kick out as hard as I can.

'Fucking bitch!' someone screams.

The thing covering my head is pulled tighter around my

neck, and I'm pushed face down onto the ground. My arms are behind me in a vice-like grip. I try fighting him off, but he's strong. One of his hands is up my skirt, then he's groping me. His grip on my arm suddenly loosens. He's trying to pull my pants down.

Gathering all my strength, I turn and knee him.

He lets out a shriek of pain.

As I pull the cloth off my face, I see him clutching his crotch. He raises his eyes to me and lunges forward. I kick him again, this time in the face. He falls back, blood streaming from his nose.

Hauling himself up, he makes a run for it, then he turns and raising his fist, shouts. 'You wait, you bitch, I'll get you for this.'

I stand transfixed, watching as he crawls through a nearby hedge. I know who it is; it's the guy from the train, the one who sat next to me.

2

BETH

EVESLY
 The Cotswolds...

Brambles from the hedgerow bite into my flesh and rip at my clothes as I force my way through trying to get him, but when I get to the other side, he's disappeared, he's nowhere in sight.

As I walk back to where it happened, I feel he's watching me, but I can't see him. My jacket and bag are still where I dropped them. I pick them up and walk back to the station.

I can't believe what just happened. I look down at my torn blouse and skirt and groan — my tights are in shreds. Anger rages through me. I want to go back and find him, but I need to change and collect Jamie from school so carry on walking.

As I walk inside the train station a couple of people stop and stare at me. A man with a half-eaten sandwich in his hand walks over to where I'm standing and peers at my face, then down at my clothes.

'Are you alright?' he asks.

I would have thought it was obvious!

I see his startled expression.

Did I say that aloud?

Cramming the rest of his sandwich into his mouth, he takes out his phone and points to a nearby bench. 'I'm the station manager. I'll call the police.'

I hesitate. I want to go home and change and if he calls the police I'll be late to collect Jamie. I'm about to say no, but he's already talking to them.

A few minutes later he walks back to where I'm standing. 'Sit down, they won't be long.'

I go to sit down and stumble. He leaps forward and grabs my arm.

'Are you okay?'

'Yes, of course,' I snap.

He takes his hand from my arm.

'I'm sorry,' I mutter. 'But I'm in a hurry, I have to...'

'Is everything alright?'

A policewoman stands staring at me with a frown on her face, then she looks at the station manager. Before I can say anything, the station manager pulls her to one side.

'Shall I call for an ambulance?' he murmurs, covering his mouth with his hand, which is ridiculous as I can hear what he's saying. The police officer just looks at him, then at me. He quickly adds. 'It looks like someone attacked her, she needs to see a doctor.'

Brushing him aside, she takes out her notebook and walks over to me. He follows.

'I want to know what happened, but first I need your name and address.'

I garble my name and address and tell her what

happened. Then there's the sound of a train. It's the next train to Oxford.

'It's my train, I have to go.'

'Don't forget to go to your local police station you'll need to sign a statement.'

I nod, run to the platform, and jump on the train.

———

As soon as I'm home, I change, then run to Jamie's school.

It's just gone three thirty when I arrive. Jamie's in the playground sitting alone on a bench.

He looks up, sees me and waves.

I run over and hug him. 'How was school?'

His face drops. 'I hate it. Can I go back to my old school?'

'But I thought you liked it.'

'I hate it Mum, I really hate it.'

Grabbing his hand, I run with him out of the school and onto the tree-lined road. 'Don't worry, it's only your second day. When you make some friends, you'll love it.'

I spot a newsagent's shop across the road with an ice cream sign outside.

'Come on, let's get an ice cream.'

We run across the road to the shop. School's forgotten for the moment, but for how long?

3

OXFORD

BACK AT MUM'S

I'M HUDDLED up on the sofa, thinking of what just happened, while Jamie's enjoying his orange juice and devouring cake.

I sit watching him. As far as he's concerned nothing's wrong, but why should there be?

I get up and stretch. I'll give Helen a call, let her know what happened, but first I'll find out what's wrong with Jamie.

'Any homework tonight?' I ask, perching myself next to him on the chair he loves to sprawl out on to watch TV.

He shrugs.

'Come on Jamie, I know something's wrong?'

He just carries on eating his cake.

'Did something happen at school today?'

Silence.

'Okay, just tell me why you don't like your new school?'

He sits scowling. 'I don't want to talk about it.'

'I know, but if you're having a hard time...'

He grunts, crams the rest of the cake into his mouth and looks at me. 'Can I watch TV?'

'Jamie, if something's wrong, you need to tell me.'

He nods, toddles off to the kitchen for another drink, comes back, props himself up on the sofa and switches on the TV.

There's not much I can do at the moment, so I get up. 'I'll call Helen then I'll get dinner ready. Okay?'

His eyes open wide. 'Are we going back to Athens?'

'No Jamie, I just want to talk to her.'

'But she said we could stay with her for a while.'

'How do you know that?'

'I heard her talking to you. I want to go back. Can we, Mum, please?'

'But you said you wanted to come here. What changed?'

He sits playing with the remote then says, 'What's for dinner?'

'I don't know. It'll be a surprise.'

As I close the door, the Star Wars theme plays.

A minute later, I'm sitting at the top of the stairs calling Helen.

Her phone rings twice, then she answers.

'Helen, it's me. I need to talk to you.'

'Beth!' she says, sounding surprised. 'You don't sound good. What's wrong?'

I don't reply.

'What happened, Beth?'

'Someone tried to rape me.'

'What!'

'Yes, Helen. Someone attacked me in broad daylight.'

She gasps. 'Are you okay?'

'Yes, I'm just so angry.'

'Do you know who it was? Did you call the police?'

'I spoke to a police officer at the train station.'

'But where did it happen?'

'Oh, it's a long story.'

'Tell me Beth, I want to know.'

'Okay, I was coming back from an interview in London. I was on the train minding my own business — the carriage was practically empty and then a guy got on and insisted on sitting next to me. Well, of course I got pissed off and moved to another seat, further down the train, then when we reached Oxford, I changed platforms and caught a train to Evesly.'

'Why were you going to Evesly?'

Oh shit, now she'll blame herself for asking me to check on her house. I get up and pace around the small landing, then look at the stairs leading to the top floor. Out of frustration, I give the stairs a kick, wishing it was him.

'Take it easy Beth, calm down, come back here for a few days, you can stay with me, I told you before...'

'How can I? Jamie just started school.'

'I had a feeling I shouldn't ask you to go to the house,' she mutters, as if to herself.

'It's not your fault Helen, the little shit must have followed me when I changed trains at Oxford. What sort of a person does that?'

Jamie comes out of the living room and looks up at me. 'When's dinner, Mum?'

'Helen, I must go. I'll call you tomorrow.'

'When's your mum coming back from Spain, Beth?'

'I'm not sure, I'll call you tomorrow...'

As I enter the kitchen my eyes fall on the half bottle of Pinot Noir sitting on the kitchen table. It's a bit early but I need a drink. Filling a small glass to the top, I gulp half of it down.

'I'm hungry Mum,' Jamie calls from the living room.

'Won't be long.'

Opening the fridge, I peer inside. There's a tub of falafel and another of hummus which he loves.

The hot rays of the sun stream through the kitchen window, so I open the back door for some fresh air, but just as I do, Mum's ginger cat Tabitha runs past me.

'Hey Tab,' I murmur, bending down to stroke her. She stares at me with her big green eyes, purring like an engine, then winds herself around my legs waiting for me to fill her bowl, which I do.

Soon the scent of cumin and mint fill the kitchen, the falafel sizzle in the pan, the salad's ready, and the pitta's in the toaster.

I'm just about to take the falafel from the pan when there's a loud crash from the living room. Tabitha jumps with fright; her ears go back. I drop the pan — it smashes to the floor.

Running into the hall, I see smoke coming from under the living room door and there's a weird crackling noise.

Jamie!

I fling the door open — flames leap into the air, and the TV looks as if it's about to explode. Jamie's on the floor. I haul him out of the room as fast as I can, then through the hallway and out of the front door onto the grass.

'What happened, Mum?' he gasps, opening his eyes.

Suddenly, our next-door neighbour Martin appears brandishing a fire extinguisher.

'Don't worry, Beth, ambulance and firefighters are en route.' He points to the fire extinguisher, 'I'll try putting it out with this.'

I nod with relief; he disappears inside the house. Jamie tries to sit up to see what's happening, then falls back.

'Don't sit up, try to relax,' I murmur, holding onto him.

A couple of minutes later, a car screeches to a halt outside our house. Out jumps a police officer. He spots me and Jamie and runs over.

Pulling out his phone, he talks to someone, then squats down beside us. 'I need to know what happened?'

'I was in the kitchen making dinner. There was an explosion.'

He nods, waiting for me to carry on.

'It happened so quickly; I ran into the hall — smoke was coming from the living room door...' I stop and look around. 'Where's the ambulance?'

He stands up. 'Don't worry, it'll be here soon.'

'But it's taking too long.'

Picking up Jamie, I run to my car.

He runs after me. 'Where are you going?'

'To the hospital.'

An ambulance siren stops me in my tracks.

The police officer looks at me, then runs over to the ambulance.

'They're over there,' he mutters to the paramedic, who nods, and runs with the police officer to where we are.

He squats down and examines Jamie. 'It's smoke inhalation,' he says, then he looks at me. 'Were you inside with him?'

'I was in the kitchen. I'm okay. It's Jamie I'm worried about.'

'You might think you're okay, but you should both be checked out.' He glances at the smoke-filled house, then at me. 'They'll probably keep him in for the night. Maybe you as well.'

'I'll stay with him if they do.'

'Good.'

The paramedic carries Jamie to the ambulance. The police officer follows along with us.

'I don't think you'll be coming back here for a while,' he says. 'You'll need to stay with friends for a few days.'

'But I don't know anyone.'

Just then Mum's neighbour Martin comes over, a look of concern on his smoke-blackened face.

'Beth, I got these for you.'

He hands me my bag and phone.

'You're lucky they were on the kitchen chair and not in the living room.'

I nod. 'Thanks Martin, I really appreciate it.'

He looks at Jamie, then back at me. 'I'll keep an eye on the house for you.'

The police officer yells at Martin to move away, then pokes his head close to mine. 'What about him? Can't you stay at his place?'

I remember Mum saying Martin had some friends from France staying with him, so shake my head. He shrugs, the ambulance doors slam shut.

When we reach the hospital, Jamie's wheeled into the accident and emergency room. He sits shivering, his face black from the smoke.

Ten minutes later a nurse comes over, looks at Jamie, then at me, and says, 'The doctor will be here soon.'

As soon as she's out of earshot Jamie grabs my arm. 'I don't want to stay here, Mum. Can we go home?'

'Don't worry, I'll be with you. They must check you, make sure you're alright.'

Shortly after, a doctor arrives and examines him.

'He's suffering from smoke inhalation,' she says. 'It's not serious, but I'm keeping him in for the night. We'll see how he is in the morning. Now let me check you out.'

After checking me out she says I'm okay.

A little later Jamie's taken to a ward and within minutes of being tucked into bed, he's fast asleep.

Propped up in a chair beside him, I sit deep in thought, then close my eyes and fall asleep for a few minutes.

A noise makes me jump. I sit listening to the sounds of the hospital — people calling out in their sleep or buzzing for a nurse.

With my head resting on my arms on the bed, I think of Athens. Things were bad in Athens and I thought we'd be safe here, but maybe we're not. First someone tries to rape me, then Mum's house bursts into flames...

'Cup of tea, love?'

Raising my head to see who it is, I see a kindly faced nurse looking at me. 'Do you take sugar?'

I shake my head.

She looks at Jamie laying peacefully in the bed. 'Don't worry, he'll be out of here tomorrow.'

Then she pours me a cup of tea. 'Drink this, it'll make you feel better. Things always seem worse at night.'

4

EVESLY - The Cotswolds
 A few days later...

WILEY AND JONAS work on a farm near Evesly. On their days off, they go to pubs to catch their prey. Sometimes they take trips on the local train, or travel from London to Oxford and then onto Evesly. It all depends on how they feel. The women they target always travel alone. They watch, then follow them. They often get lucky. Their victims are usually young and too scared to go to the police. They know what will happen if they do.

Wiley frowns, screws up his watery pale blue eyes and touches his sore face.

After it happened, he watched her go back to the train station in Evesly. With all that blood pouring from his face, how could he follow her? He called Jonas - told him what she looked like and to get a cab to Evesly station, follow her and find out where she lived.

He smiles, thinking of what he did to her, then scowls, touches his face and mutters, 'She'll suffer for this'.

As he picks up the local newspaper to check the racing results, a headline catches his eye.

LOCAL WOMAN ATTACKED IN FIELD

He sits reading the article, chortling to himself, but then gets to the bit about the attacker's description.

He re-reads the article and screams with rage. 'She's only gone and given the police my description.'

Jonas laughs. 'What ya gonna do?'

Wiley stomps around the room cursing, then locks eyes with Jonas. 'The bitch, I'm going to kill her. I'll have to buy new clothes, make myself look different.'

'Don't be a dickhead. I don't believe in killing. Do all the other stuff but not murder.'

'You're the dickhead,' snarls Wiley, tearing the page from the paper and screwing it into a ball.

A sly smile spreads over Jonas's face. 'Don't worry — you'll get her back in other ways. She's one of those women...'

'Shut up!'

Wiley thumps his fist so hard on the table his coffee cup falls over.

'Bitch! Fucking bitch!'

His face contorts with rage.

Then he sees the coffee dripping off the table, and throws the newspaper over it.

Then he catches sight of his reflection in the living room mirror and hurls an ashtray at the mirror.

Glaring at Jonas he runs to the front door, wrenches it

open and stands staring ahead of him. His face is red and blotchy, his blood pressure high.

Jonas takes his eyes off the TV screen to watch him. 'Where ya going?'

Wiley slams the door behind him.

Jonas goes back to watching TV.

SOME TIME LATER, Wiley returns with bags of shopping, and disappears into the bathroom.

An hour later he emerges. 'What d'ya think?' he asks, parading in front of Jonas.

His long greasy, limp brown hair is now platinum blond.

'What the fuck!' Jonas eyes him up and down, then sniggers. 'You look like a woman. The blokes at work will think you've lost it.'

Wiley grabs Jonas' packet of weed, runs to the toilet and empties it down the toilet. 'Now who's laughing, wanker?'

Jonas sits looking stunned.

Wiley returns to the bathroom.

NOT LONG AFTER, Wiley returns to the living room and saunters over to Jonas.

'I look good, don't I?'

His limp long blond hair has small gelled blond spikes sticking out all over his head.

Jonas takes one look at him and runs from the living room into the bathroom, laughing and clutching his pants.

Wiley just ignores him and grabs his new clothes.

Off come the faded blue low waist jeans, and on come the tight skinny leather trousers. A slow smile spreads over his pockmarked face as he surveys himself in the smashed mirror.

'She thinks she's so clever,' he mutters, clenching his fists.

Then narrowing his cold, watery blue eyes he licks his lips. 'She won't feel so clever the next time we meet.'

5

OXFORD HOSPITAL
7.43 am next morning

It's early morning and already the hospital's a hive of activity. Thankfully, Jamie's a lot better than he was last night. His appetite's good, so he should be leaving this morning.

Then I need to check the house to see how bad the living room is, and get it cleaned up, then go to the police station in Evesly, make a statement and find out what started the fire.

A young, dark-haired police officer suddenly appears on the ward. She talks to one of the nurses for a couple of minutes, then walks over to me.

'Good morning, I'm PC Hamilton. We need to talk about finding you somewhere to stay.'

She looks at Jamie, then back at me. 'Don't worry, he'll be alright. I've asked the nurse to come and stay with him.'

A nurse comes over, puffs up Jamie's pillows and gives

him a smile. 'Let's get you ready for the doctor. See if you can go home today. You'd like that, wouldn't you?'

Jamie's eyes light up at the sound of going home. The nurse smiles and takes his temperature.

I give him a wave. 'Be back in a minute.'

Then I follow the PC into a small room outside the ward.

She sits down at a desk and points to the chair opposite.

'Do you have any news about the fire?' I ask, sitting down and watching as she flicks through her phone.

'Sorry, but I'm only here to discuss accommodation.'

'But surely you can...'

'You'll have to ask at the station,' she replies briskly. 'Now, is there someone you can stay with for a couple of days?'

'No, we've only been here a few days. My mother's on holiday. I know the living room's a mess, but I don't think the fire reached the upstairs bedrooms.'

'Well, we have to make sure it's safe before you can return.'

'Can you find out, please?'

She nods. 'It often looks worse than it is. I'll speak to one of my colleagues and see what they say.'

'Thanks.'

A few minutes later, she closes her phone and smiles. 'You're in luck. The kitchen and top floors of the house are okay. The forensics team has finished, so you can go back if you like, but keep the windows open to ventilate the place.'

She pockets her phone, then hands me a card. 'Call me if you need anything.'

She stands as if to go, then turns and looks at me. 'I believe you're due to make an official statement at the station tomorrow?'

I nod and slip her card into my pocket.

'If you have any concerns, you can discuss them with the detective in charge of the case. I think it's Detective Chief Inspector Thomas.'

'Thanks, I'll contact him as soon as we get out of here.'

She leaves and I return to the ward.

Still no doctor, so I go in search of a strong cup of coffee for me, and a chocolate bar for Jamie.

When I return, I'm relieved to see the doctor's with him. She looks up. 'Your son's much better today. We just have to finish the paperwork, then he can go home.'

Jamie's over the moon. I call a cab.

On the way home, he's silent. He's probably thinking of what happened last night. Then I think of what used to be Mum's lovely living room.

Is she insured?

'We're nearly there, Mum,' says Jamie.

A few minutes later the taxi screeches to a halt. Jamie leaps out and runs to the house, then shouts for me to go over.

I search for some change to pay the driver, then see Jamie running back to the cab. He looks flustered.

'There's a police officer in our garden,' he pants.

I follow his gaze and sure enough, a young police officer is watching us. The taxi driver raises an eyebrow, gives me a knowing wink, then drives off.

'What the hell is he doing here?' I groan. 'I thought they'd gone.'

'Is anything wrong?' I ask, walking over to the officer.

'It's orders. I thought you knew. There's an officer at the back as well.'

I'm speechless. I wouldn't have thought they'd have the budget for even one officer, let alone two.

Jamie follows me into the house.

We pass the blackened door of the living room.

I'll look at it later when Jamie's in bed.

Jamie looks out of the kitchen window, then at me. 'Why are they here, Mum?'

'I'm not sure, but they won't be here for long.'

I'm amazed they're here, I nearly add, but don't.

He looks very glum, so I quickly add, 'At least we still have the garden to sit in.'

He stares at the young officer at the end of the back garden. 'But we can't sit in the garden with him over there, can we?'

'Don't worry, I'll sort something out. Now let's have something to drink.'

He stands frowning, then looks over to the living room door. 'Do you think it'll happen again?'

'No, of course not. The police will soon find out what happened.'

He looks at me in surprise. 'But I saw it. It came through the window. Someone threw it.'

Even though I had a feeling it wasn't faulty electrics, I feel shocked to hear him say this.

'I wish you'd mentioned this earlier, Jamie.'

'Sorry, I thought you knew.'

I hug him to me. 'Don't worry, it was probably a couple of kids larking about and their homemade fire-bomb ended up in our living room.'

He gives me one of his looks, as if to say — you must be joking. It's times like this he reminds me of his dad. He's only eleven years old, well, nearly twelve, but he looks young for his age.

A pitiful meow from the back door makes us both jump.

Jamie runs to open it, scoops Mum's ginger cat up into

his arms, and gives her a big hug. Tabitha meows happily and nuzzles her head against him.

'We're not staying here, are we Mum?' Jamie mutters.

'Of course not, we'll get something to eat.'

His face brightens up. 'Can we go to McDonald's?'

I laugh. 'Yes, now go and have a shower.'

He runs upstairs. I feed Tabitha.

When we leave, Tabitha's watching from the bedroom window, probably hoping we won't forget to come back and feed her. I suddenly shiver and look back at the house. I need to find out who did this.

6

Next morning...

I'M IN THE GARDEN, thinking of Mum. I don't want to ruin her holiday, but I must tell her what's happened...I press her number.

'Hi Mum, how are you?'

'Beth, what a surprise, I'm fine. How are you?'

'Listen Mum, I have something to tell you.'

She says nothing, so I continue.

'There's been a fire at the house, but it's okay now.'

'A fire? What sort of fire?'

'The living room's a bit of a mess, but the rest of the house is okay.'

'But how did it start?'

So, I tell her just as much as I need to.

'Are you okay?' she gasps.

'Yes, of course, don't worry Mum, we're both okay. I'm sure the police will sort it out soon.'

She pauses for a few minutes. 'Okay, I'll book a flight. I'll be home tonight.'

I knew she'd say this.

'No, finish your holiday. I'll get the living room cleaned up.'

Then I remember the insurance.

'Mum, do you have insurance?'

'I'm not sure if my house insurance covers this. I'll have to find out.'

'Can I help?'

'No, I'll call them. You go online and get some tickets to Palma. Let me know when you're arriving. I'll be at the airport to meet you.'

Of course, she's right. How can Jamie stay here?

'Okay, but I'm staying here. I'll clean up the living room, get some new furniture...'

'Are you crazy, Beth? What are you going to do? Let the police deal with it.'

'I need to find a job, Mum. I'll stay here, get this place sorted, and don't forget Tabitha. Someone has to be here to look after her.'

She's silent for a minute. 'Do you remember Nick from school in Evesly?'

Now it's my turn to be surprised. 'What has he got to do with it? I haven't seen him since we were at school.'

'Call him, tell him what happened.' Then she mutters something I don't quite catch.

'What did you say, Mum?'

'I said if he doesn't know already. Now promise me you'll call him.'

'But I haven't seen him for years,' I groan. 'How on earth can he help?'

Word gets around quickly in a village like Evesly. It

always does in these small Cotswold villages, and it's not as if Nick and I were close when we were at school.'

'He can help Beth, and he still lives in Evesly.'

'Yes, okay, I'll call him. Now I must go. I have to let Jamie's school know what's happened.'

Schools hate parents taking kids out during term time. In fact, the government passed a law in the UK banning it, but this is different. He's not going on holiday to have fun.

'Okay, let me know when his flight is and tell him not to worry.'

After saying goodbye to Mum, I key in the school's number. I'm put through to the head-teacher and I was right, she isn't pleased.

'But he's only been here two days!'

'Yes, I know, but this is an emergency. You can check with the police.'

I feel terrible doing this. We were lucky to get him in at the last minute.

She's not happy but finally agrees. 'Alright, but don't make it too long. Keep me up to date with what's happening.'

'Yes, of course. As soon as I know anything, I'll call you.'

I check on-line for flights, then realise

I must check about children flying alone. Iberia, the Spanish airline, says the child must be twelve years old to fly alone.

He'll be twelve this month, I wonder…

I search Google for information; it says I can request an escort service for minors at the same time as the booking. I have twenty-four hours to do this and then there's a list of things I must do.

I skim through them, then check for flights.

There's a flight leaving tomorrow morning at 11.45 — I've just enough time.

A few minutes later, Jamie's flight's booked, I've completed the form, then I'm off upstairs to tell Jamie.

'I HEARD you talking in the garden,' he growls, peering at me over the top of his duvet.

His bedroom window's slightly ajar, which is strange as I always check the windows. It was closed when we went to bed.

'Did you open the window last night?' I ask as I go over to the bed and puff up his duvet.

'No, I don't think so. I don't remember, maybe I did. It was hot last night.'

He looks worried, so I sit down on the bed and ruffle his hair. 'Cheer up! I just spoke to your headteacher. She said it's alright for you to have a few days off so you're going to stay with Nan in Spain for a couple of weeks. She said it's lovely there, you can...'

'But I want you to come. You can't stay here on your own.'

'Oh Jamie, I want to come but someone's got to stay here and sort things out.'

He snorts and buries his head in the duvet.

'The flight crew will look after you, so there's no need to worry. I've sorted it all out.'

He covers himself with the duvet. 'If I have to go anywhere, I'd rather go to Athens.'

'Look, I know it's difficult. You miss your friends, but Nan will take you to the beach every day. You can go swimming, play football.'

He sits up in bed, props his face in his hands and looks at me. 'Okay, but I'm not going back to that school.'

'We'll talk about that later. Now, have a quick shower and I'll make breakfast.'

When he's safely in the shower, I run downstairs to call Helen. No reply.

A few minutes later, Jamie comes down the stairs, showing off the new jeans we bought yesterday.

'What shall we do after breakfast?' I ask, pouring him a juice.

He sits thinking for a minute, then his eyes light up. 'What about a Harry Potter tour? We can see Hogwarts. Let's go there?'

'Okay, let's have breakfast first, then we'll go.'

'Yay, cool! What's for breakfast?'

I sigh with relief. We'll have a good time today, tomorrow he'll go to Spain, then I'll contact the police.

7

Jamie goes to Spain...

THE DRIVE to the airport's usually a happy event, but today we're both quiet. I'm worried. It's his first time flying alone. He says he's looking forward to it, but I'm not so sure. I peek at him from the corner of my eye. He catches me looking and grins.

'Don't worry Mum, I'll be okay.'

I turn the radio on and focus on the road ahead. Fortunately, there's not too much traffic and we're soon at the airport.

After completing all the documentation, Jamie's taken through the security gate. He doesn't seem at all bothered. In fact, I think he's enjoying it.

Tears fill my eyes — he looks so small — I give him a wave, then he's gone.

Twenty minutes later, the plane takes off. I leave the airport, locate my car, and drive home.

On the way back, my phone rings, I ignore it. I'm driving, they can leave a message. As I drive home, all I can see is Jamie sitting on that plane. He didn't seem bothered about going by himself. I just want him to be safe. I eventually convince myself he's okay, he has his phone; he can always call me when he lands.

―――

GOING BACK HOME without Jamie is strange. The place is so empty. The police officers in the front garden as usual, and the other one's still around the back.

I keep thinking of Jamie on that plane alone.

What will happen if Mum doesn't get there in time?

Grabbing my phone, I call Mum.

'Yes, Beth, I'm on my way to the airport, and I have plenty of time, so don't stress and stop thinking about him sitting on the plane all by himself.'

'I can't help it Mum, it's the first time he's flown without me.'

'I know, but the flight doesn't take that long and by the time he's had something to eat, it'll be time to land.'

'Okay, call me when he lands.'

'Yes, Beth, now take care of yourself.'

'I will Mum.'

After a small glass of wine, I remember someone called when I was driving back. I look at my phone. There's a message from Nick. He wants me to call him.

How on earth did Nick get my number?

I listen to the message. His voice sounds deeper than I remember, stronger, more confident. Well, of course it would. The last time I saw him, he was only seventeen.

Tossing my phone onto the small garden table, I sit on one of the old benches, contemplating my plan of action. I'll contact the police first, find out if they've caught whoever did this, and then I'll…

My phone rings. It's Nick.

'Beth, how are you?'

'Nick, what a surprise. How are you?'

'I'm okay, but more to the point, how are you?'

Of course, he knows all about it, either Mum told him or he heard about it through the grapevine. News travels fast in Evesly.

'Nick, it's very nice of you to call, but you really don't have to worry. There are two police officers guarding the house.'

'Okay, but I still want to see you. We've got a lot of catching up to do.'

Seeing Nick is the last thing I need right now. 'I'm sorry, Nick, but it's not a good time. I'll call you later.'

'Beth, I know all about it. Your mother told me — I know someone attacked you and I want to help. Can I come over tonight after work?'

I had a feeling he might know about the fire, but only Helen knows about that bastard attacking me and she wouldn't go blabbing her mouth off to Mum.

'Sorry Nick, I must go. I'll call you later.'

My mind's racing. How did Mum find out? Only the police know and the station manager.

Then I have a thought.

Oh, no! Grabbing my purse, I run the few yards to the local shop. Nothing much has changed. The old black cat's still fast asleep under the newspaper stand, and inside, next to the till, are the free local newspapers.

As I take one from the top of the pile, the guy behind the counter gives me a strange look.

Is there something inside about me? Am I being paranoid?

He goes back to serving the kids sweets. I go outside.

A small heading on the second page catches my eye.

WOMAN ATTACKED IN EVESLY

I quickly scan through it, then stop. They've printed a description of me. One of Mum's mates must have seen this and called her. Mum will know it's me. She's not stupid.

Folding the paper up, I shove it into my bag and leave the shop.

BACK AT HOME I sit re-reading the article, then my phone rings. It's the police.

Shit, I was supposed to see them today.

I arrange to see them tomorrow, then there's a tap at the door, then another.

I sit with my arms propped up on the table holding my head, hoping they'll go away, but they don't.

There's another tap, this time much louder.

Now they're really pissing me off. Who the hell knocks like that?

Tripping over one of Jamie's shoes, I run to the door.

'Yes?' I growl, flinging the door open.

'Sorry, I didn't mean to interrupt, but as I was in the area...'

He stands staring at me.

Is he selling something?

He's quite tall, dark hair, tanned, very well built. I shake my head and mumble something about being busy and start closing the door.

'Beth. It's me. Don't you recognize me?'

Then I know who it is, but he's changed, really changed.

8

'Nick, I didn't recognize you. What have you done to yourself?'

He laughs and stands looking at me. 'You haven't changed. Your hair's longer, but it suits you.'

We stand staring at each other for a minute, then I laugh. 'It's so lovely to see you. Do you want to come in?'

He nods. 'Yes, I'd love to.'

As we pass the blackened living room door, he pauses slightly. I ignore it and walk into the kitchen. 'It's such a lovely day. Let's sit outside in the garden.'

The police officer at the end of the garden sees us coming and quickly stubs out his cigarette. I point to the bench next to the table.

Nick sits down.

'I was just about to cook a pizza. Are you hungry?'

He nods. 'Sounds great. Can I help?'

'No, stay here. I won't be long.'

I shove the pizza in the microwave, then realize I didn't ask him what he'd like to drink.

Opening the window, I shout. 'Nick, beer or coke?'

He looks up from his phone. 'Beer would be great. Are you sure I can't help?'

I smile and shake my head. 'No, stay there, enjoy the garden.'

Beer, he wants beer. Do we have any?

Quickly, I rummage around in the fridge—but there's no beer!

Where the hell does Mum keep the beer? Maybe he'd like some wine?

Then I spy some bottles of San Miguel stuffed under the salad stuff alongside a bottle of Prosecco.

Quickly popping it open, I take it outside.

As soon as he sees me, he stops chatting to the police officer at the end of the garden, walks over, and takes the beer.

'Thanks, Beth.'

I give him a smile. I feel awkward. I haven't seen him for years and this isn't the Nick I remember, the shy, skinny boy with the doleful brown eyes.

Then I hear the microwave ting from the kitchen.

His brown eyes twinkle. 'Can I help?'

'No, stay here, I'll get it.'

As I place the pizza on a plate, I watch him from the window. I still can't believe how much he's changed.

Grabbing the pizza cutter from the drawer, I take it outside, slice it up, pop a couple of slices on a plate, and pass it to him.

'I hope you like mozzarella and pesto.'

There's a slight smile on his face. 'It's one of my favorites.'

He bites into a slice. 'Very good, Beth.'

Suddenly, he reaches over and puts his hand over mine.

'Beth, I want to help. If you remember anything about the guy who attacked you, please tell me.'

I nearly choke on my pizza; he hands me his beer.

What did Mum say he does for a living? I'm sure he studied law, but that was a long time ago.

'I'm a DI, a Detective Inspector,' he murmurs, as if reading my mind. 'Didn't your mother tell you?' Now this has shocked me, and he knows it.

He laughs and carries on talking. 'I work for the police. I studied law; don't you remember? I always found criminal law interesting and with my new job...'

He stops to light a cigarette, inhales deeply and carries on. 'I get to see things first-hand, if you know what I mean.'

I nod. 'Yes, but I never thought you'd end up working for the police.'

He takes out his cigarettes. 'Sorry, I forgot to offer you one. Do you smoke?'

'No thanks.'

My mind's racing. He's a detective. It would be easy for him to find out about my case - the attack, the fire. Maybe he already knows?

'Nick, let's go inside. I'll make some coffee.'

'Sure.' He stubs out his cigarette and follows me into the kitchen.

While I'm filling up the kettle, he picks up a framed photo of Mum, me, and Jamie.

'So, when did you get divorced?' he asks, looking closely at the photo.

Mum really has been busy - I wonder how much she told him. 'It's just going through. It will probably take a couple more weeks.'

Placing the photo carefully back on the sideboard, he suddenly smiles. 'Then you'll be a free woman.'

'Yes, I suppose so. I haven't really thought about it - it happened so quickly.'

Why am I telling him this? I haven't seen him for years.

He's looking at me so strangely.

'Don't worry, Beth, I'm sure you'll be alright. I was married for a couple of years, but it didn't work out either, not as long as you, of course.' He glances back at the photo.

'Your son has green eyes just like yours. How old is he?'

'He's nearly twelve.'

He stands watching me — he looks older, more confident, but there's something else.

'You know, the last thing I heard about you was that you'd married a Greek, you were having a ball in Athens.' He stops and frowns. 'Sorry, I shouldn't have said that. I didn't think, how stupid of me.'

'Don't worry, you haven't upset me. I may not look it, but I've toughened up over the years.'

He raises an eyebrow and laughs. 'I don't think so. You still look the same as you did when you were seventeen, or was it eighteen when you went back to Greece?'

'You'd be surprised Nick. Appearances can be deceptive.'

If only he knew - he'd probably run a mile. I've changed so much, even I don't recognize myself sometimes. Then I think of my Glock 17 stored away with most of my things in a locked room in our apartment in Athens. I thought I'd be safe here, but now I'm not so sure.

'Milk and sugar, Nick?'

'Black, no sugar, thanks.'

He sits down at the table. I bring over the coffee.

'Nick, about my case, do you think... are these incidents connected?'

He's just about to say something when his phone rings.

'Sorry, I'll take it outside.'

He gets up and walks out of the kitchen into the garden.

I sit drinking my coffee thinking about Nick.

A few minutes later, he's back.

'Beth, I have to go. It's something urgent. Can I call you tomorrow?'

'Yes, of course.'

I stand watching him drive away in his shiny black VW Golf. Well, what a surprise that was.

My phone rings. It's Mum.

'Hi Mum, how are you? How's Jamie?'

'I'm fine, and so is Jamie. He can't wait to tell you about his flight. I just wish you were here. He really misses you. Have you heard from the police?'

'No, but I have heard from Nick. He just came to see me. You didn't tell me he works for the police.'

She grunts. 'Good, let's hope he can help. Now talk to Jamie.'

I can hear her talking to him, then he's on the phone.

'Mum, it's great here. When are you coming?'

I can't help but laugh. It's so good to hear his voice. 'Jamie, I told you, I'll be there in a couple of days. Now tell me about your flight.'

When we've finished, I sit looking at my phone. I know Mum will look after him, but I'm worried. What happens when they come back? What if the police haven't found out who did this?

We're running low on wine, so I decide to take a walk to the supermarket. It'll clear my head, help me think.

As I get near the shops, my phone rings. It's Nick.

'Beth, I really don't think you should walk around Oxford by yourself.'

I stop dead in my tracks. Did that young police officer call him? I saw him watching me when I left the house.

'How do you know where I am?'

He totally ignores me and starts prattling on about a pub in the high street.

'Listen, there's a small pub, three doors along from Tesco. I'll be there in ten minutes.'

9

BETH & NICK

OXFORD

I'M NEARLY at Tesco's when I see the pub he's talking about. It's a typical old-style English pub which I remember coming too many times when I was younger. Low beams, smells of beer, it's all very quaint.

As soon as I enter, the barman stops talking to the man at the bar and glances over at me.

'Yes, m'dear, can I help you?'

I'd forgotten how friendly old English pubs are and walk over to the bar, place a ten-pound note in front of him and smile. 'Two halves of lager, please.'

The barman nods. I look around for somewhere to sit.

'There's a seat over there,' the barman calls, pointing to a table by the window. 'I'll bring them over.'

'Thanks.'

It's a small table for two, with wood carved chairs next to a window looking out onto the high street. The chair is surprisingly sturdy and very comfortable. The windows are tiny; they look Elizabethan. I peer through one of them and see Nick. He's on his phone, hurrying towards the pub.

The barman brings over the beers, gives me my change, then ambles back to the bar.

Nick's quite tall, so to avoid hitting his head on the beams, he has to duck when he comes inside.

'It's a lovely old pub. Is this your local?' I ask, moving my chair to give him some room.

He laughs. 'I often pop in for a quick drink. It's very handy and the beer's good.' Then his voice changes. He looks worried. 'You shouldn't be out alone, Beth, after what happened.'

I can't believe he just said that. I know I must be vigilant, but for him to say I shouldn't go out is ridiculous.

'I'm not staying at home just because some nutter firebombed our house. What planet do you live on, Nick?'

A muscle twitches in his cheek. He says nothing, but I can see I've hit a nerve.

'Nick, you said you want to help, and I really need your help. Has this sort of thing happened before? Are there many cases like this?'

He doesn't reply, just leans back in his chair, stretches his legs out under the table and sips his beer.

'Nick,' I almost shout, then lower my voice. 'I can't put my life on hold. I have a son to look after. They could have killed him. We must find them before they try doing it again. Nick, this is serious, you must help.'

He straightens up, puts his elbows on the table, and stares at me. 'Beth, this is all being taken care of by the police.'

'But they haven't arrested the person who did this, have they?'

'We will. You must be patient, Beth.'

He sits gazing at me. I frown. 'And what about the CCTV footage? I need to see this as soon as possible. If I can identify the man, then you'll know who attacked me.'

He sighs, wraps his hand over mine in a friendly way, and smiles. 'The police will ask you to come in and see if you recognize anyone, but first you must make an official statement. Have you been to the station?'

I shake my head. 'No, I'll do it tomorrow. I was busy taking Jamie to the airport, and then you came round.'

We sit silently drinking our beer. He's looking at his phone. I'm racking my brains trying to think what else I must ask him. Then I remember.

'Nick, do you know if there's any CCTV in our street? I looked, but I can't see any.'

He shakes his head. 'I wouldn't think so, but you never know. I'll check tomorrow.'

'And don't forget to find out if there have been any similar cases in the area. It will give us something to go on.'

He's just about to say something, then he shrugs. 'I'll try, but I can't promise you anything. Now drink up, I've an early start tomorrow. I must be up at 5.30 and you look as if you could do with a good sleep. My car's just around the corner.'

Ten minutes later, we're outside Mum's house. I slide out of the car and close the door.

'Thanks, Nick.'

I can feel him watching me as I walk to the front door.

'I'll call you tomorrow,' he calls, then drives off.

The house feels empty, slightly creepy. It's a warm night, but I shiver. I switch on all the lights, go into the kitchen, pull the blinds down, and open the back door.

Tabitha usually comes running inside as soon as the lights go on. 'Tab, where are you?' No Tabitha, how strange.

Upstairs I look under the beds, but there's no sign of her.

I'm getting worried. She's always very punctual with her food.

I take a quick peek outside the back door, but still no Tabitha. Mum installed a cat flap, so she can always use that. Maybe she's having too much fun to think of food. It's a lovely night, so good luck to her. I close the door and start making a pot of tea. I'll watch the ten o'clock news, then go to bed.

As I'm filling the kettle, I suddenly hear a strange tapping noise.

Turning the tap off, I listen. There it goes again - tap, tap, tap.

10

BETH

Next morning...

I STILL DON'T UNDERSTAND why Nick didn't call? He has my number. How was I supposed to know it was him outside tapping on the window, and who taps on a window like that? He's the one saying I should be careful.

Then he shouted through the letterbox, 'Beth, you left your purse in the car.'

After that I couldn't sleep. I drank a glass of red wine then ended up finishing the bottle, staggered upstairs, collapsed into bed and now feel like shit.

Two large strong black coffees later I'm in Evesly.

After driving around for ten minutes, I eventually find somewhere to park and go to the police station. This may be a sleepy little village, but the folks here get up very early.

Inside the station, an officer gives me a cursory glance and asks if he can help me.

'Yes,' I reply, more chirpily than I feel. 'I'm here to make a statement. My name is Beth...'

Suddenly the door behind him opens, a man walks out, he has a kindly-looking face.

He stands, eyeing me up and down. 'You must be Beth Papadakis?' I nod.

'I'm Detective Chief Inspector Thomas. They told me you were coming. Please follow me.'

I follow him to a room, and after making my statement, he mutters. 'Follow me. I have some photos for you to look at. Hopefully, you'll recognise that man who attacked you.'

'Do you have the results of the samples taken from our living room?'

He shakes his head.

'But I'm sure someone in forensics said it only takes a couple of days.'

He pushes up his glasses, turns and looks at me. 'Not yet. These things take time. Now let's see if you recognise that man who attacked you.'

As we enter the room, I'm surprised to see just a handful of photos stacked up on a table, all ready for me to look through.

I flick through them, but none of them resemble the guy on the train.

DCI Thomas just looks out of the window, waiting for me to finish.

Walking over to where he's standing, I ask. 'None of them look like him. Do you have anymore?' He swings round and gazes at me.

'Are you sure? Why not have another look?'

Is he serious? There are only six photos and none of them look at all like the guy who tried to rape me.

I give him a steely look. 'No, I'm sure. So, what happens now?'

'Forensics will test the samples; we'll be in touch.'

'And how long will that take?'

He gives me an irritated look and starts walking out of the room. 'We'll be in touch, now if you'll excuse me...'

I'm so angry, I have to stop myself from charging after him, but what's the point? It'll only make things worse.

Out of the corner of my eye I suddenly see Nick, he's talking to someone. Maybe he has some news. I decide to hang around. There's nothing much to look at, so I just stand looking out of the window.

After a few minutes, I turn and catch him looking at me. He mumbles something to the man he's with, then beckons me over.

As the man passes me, his cold grey eyes bore into me.

'Who was that?' I ask, turning to look at the retreating figure.

Nick laughs and takes me by the arm. 'That's Major Oliver Hudson, he's really nice, he owns a farm in Evesly, he's an MP, works mostly in London, but he's often in the village. He used to be in the army, lived in Cyprus.'

'He's here on business or just a friendly visit?'

Nick gives me a surprised look and taps his nose, as if to say it's none of my business. 'Now let's not waste any more time talking about the major. Did you look at any mugshots?'

'I didn't recognise any of them.'

He raises an eyebrow.

'Nick, there were only six photos. Surely you have more.'

'Obviously not. This is a small village, Beth.'

'Well, it's nice to know there's not much crime happening here, but what about the CCTV footage from the train? Can I look at that?'

He gives me a funny look. 'The police are working as fast

as they can. You must be patient. I'll let you know when we have it.'

I'm about to reply when my phone rings. It's Mum.

'Okay, I've got to go - I'll talk to you later.'

I can feel his eyes burning into my back as I leave the room.

No wonder nothing gets done in this place; they're all too busy hobnobbing with the local gentry.

Then I think of the Major, a nasty-looking man, an MP, a member of parliament. Whoever elected him needs their brains tested.

I'm nearly home when my phone rings. It's Nick. I let it go to voicemail.

It rings again. He leaves a message for me to call him, says it's important.

Later, after I've eaten some pizza and had a couple of glasses of wine, I switch on my phone. Ten missed calls, all from Nick, plus another message.

I forgot to tell you, the Major's holding a charity ball tomorrow and you're invited—let me know if you want to come.

Why would the Major invite me to his ball? He doesn't even know me.

11

HELEN

ATHENS
10.15 pm in the evening

GRABBING an ice-cold beer from the fridge, I open the French windows and inhale the scent of the warm summer evening.

The heat from the day still lingers in the streets of Athens, the heavy scent of jasmine clings to the night air. It's the perfect time to go for a stroll, but I'm tired. I started work at 7.30 this morning and now it's 10.15 in the evening so I'm hot and exhausted. I stand sipping my beer while gazing at the Parthenon. It's a lovely sight any time of the day, but tonight it looks more beautiful than usual.

Then I think of Beth. She used to sit gazing at it for hours as if it hypnotized her. If only I hadn't asked her to visit the house none of this would have happened. I should've let the estate agent deal with it.

I sit down, light a cigarette, and inhale deeply. I know

she can take care of herself, but I'm worried. All I can think of is the man who attacked her. Why the hell did I ask her to check on the house?

The house phone rings. It's my husband, Theo. He says not to wait up for him. He does this practically every night, so I'm used to it. Then it hits me. I shouldn't be here worrying about Beth. I should be in Oxford with her.

I rummage through my bag for my phone. I'll book a flight to London. A few days in Oxford will give me enough time to convince Beth that it's time to come back. I'm sure Tula can take care of things at the travel agency for a few days. She often helps me out when I'm busy and I know she needs the money.

As soon as I've booked my ticket, I call Tula, no reply. I leave a message, telling her I'm going to Oxford for a few days and to call me. She has the keys to the office, so it shouldn't be a problem. If it is, it'll just have to stay closed for a few days.

A couple of hours later, I call Tula. I'm in luck. She was late getting back from the islands and can take care of the office for a few days.

I throw a few things into a small bag for the morning, then go to bed. If I call Beth, she'll tell me not to come. She'll say she's fine, but I know she isn't. I'll send her an email, then she won't be able to stop me.

THEO DIDN'T COME HOME last night. He often does this when he drinks too much. He probably slept at his club. I scribble him a note about where I'm going, pin it onto the fridge and leave.

I was going to take a taxi to the airport, but it might be

quicker to go by train as the roads are busy now. My flight leaves in just over an hour. I must hurry.

Running down the steps of the metro, I pause. Is someone calling me?

Swinging round, I see Theo, my husband, running towards me.

'Where do you think you're going?' he shouts, clenching his fists angrily.

I put my hand up to shade my eyes from the early morning sun and gaze at his angry face.

'Theo, I have a plane to catch. I'll call you later.'

As I turn to leave, he runs down and grabs me by the arm. 'No, you don't. You're coming back with me.'

The arguments have become worse over the past few months. They always end the same. He says he's working hard to make money for me. What a joke.

People are staring at us. I lean forward so they won't hear me. 'What's wrong with you, Theo? I'm going to see Beth. Now let go of my arm.'

But he won't let go, his breath stinks of alcohol. I don't want him to cause a scene, but the state he's in other than calling the police, what can I do?

I run up the metro steps, walk the ten minutes back to the house with him, open the front door and go inside.

'This has got to stop!' I shout. 'I told you what happened to Beth. What's wrong with you? You stay out practically every night, then come home reeking of alcohol. How dare you!'

He pushes me into the living room and starts screaming like a lunatic. 'Don't talk to me like that, ever!' Then he prods me with his finger. 'You're staying here.'

I give him a shove, which sends him flying onto the sofa. He's so drunk, but he pulls himself up. He sways, then staggers and lunges towards me. My hand hovers over an onyx ornament on a nearby table. If he comes near me again, I swear I'll smash it over his head.

It's as if he knows what I'm thinking because he suddenly turns and flops down on the sofa, sits holding his head in his hands and groans. 'You know I love you, I'll ...'

HIS HEAD FALLS FORWARD. He's asleep.

Closing the front door gently, I run as fast as I can to the metro. On the way, my phone rings but I don't have time to answer it.

At last, I'm at the station, it's rush hour. I squeeze into a carriage, but there's nowhere to sit, so I stand all the way to the airport.

Feeling hot and sticky, I leave the train and run to departures. It's the last call the boarding gates are closing.

They see me running and wait, then usher me through the gates.

I stumble onto the plane, locate my seat and two minutes later we take-off.

12

BETH

OXFORD
Early afternoon

I'M HUNCHED over my laptop searching all the local news websites for assaults and arson attacks in the Evesly area and I've found zilch, nada.

A bottle of Pinot Noir on the kitchen shelf catches my eye. It's very tempting, but I must keep my wits about me. Instead, I make a cup of strong black coffee to keep me going.

My phone rings. It's Helen.

'Hi Beth, I've just landed at Gatwick. I'll see you soon.'

'Helen!'

Coffee spurts from my mouth. 'But I sent you a text. Didn't you get it?'

She laughs. 'I didn't get it. I was in the air. Anyway, I'm here now.'

I glimpse myself in the kitchen mirror and groan. My hair needs washing, the place is a mess and there's no food.

Suddenly, the house phone rings.

'Helen, the house phone is ringing. It might be the police. I must answer it.'

'Of course you must. See you soon.' There's a click, and she's gone.

I grab the house phone. It's Nick.

'Beth, I've been trying to get hold of you. Can I come around?'

'What's so urgent?' I snap. 'I really don't have time, Helen's...'

'I'll tell you when I get there.'

A few minutes later, his car skids to a halt outside our house.

'Give me your phone,' he asks as soon as I open the front door. He pushes past me into the kitchen and holds out his hand. He looks flustered. I wonder what's happened?

'Why do you want it?'

'Just give it to me, Beth.'

He stands glaring at me, taps his hand nervously on the chair in front of him, and frowns. 'Come on Beth, it's just to be on the safe side, in case...'

'In case what? Has something happened?'

He shakes his head. 'No, but I need to fit you with a tracking device.'

'So, something has happened?'

He shakes his head impatiently. 'Come on Beth, I haven't got all day.'

My mobile's on the table. He spots it, picks it up, and opens it. I walk around the table so I can see what he's doing. 'What aren't you telling me, Nick?

'Like I said, it's just to be on the safe side. You must stay inside. It's only for a few days - I'm sure you can manage that.'

He points to the garden. 'Make yourself useful, plant some vegetables or flowers.' Then he looks over towards the living room door. 'There's a lot you can do in there, clean it up, paint the walls and if you really need to go out, call me and I'll take you.'

Something's wrong; it's written all over his face, then I think of Helen. 'Well, if you really want to help.'

He looks at me and groans. 'Beth, I'm working. I can't take you out now.'

'I'm not joking — the fridge is empty. Helen's coming. I must do a food shop and get some drinks in.'

Disbelief is written all over his face. 'Surely you knew she was coming? You must have something in the fridge?'

'If I knew she was coming I would've gone shopping or done an online shop, wouldn't I? She just called me from the airport, so I have to go out.' Then, just in case he's forgotten who Helen is, I add. 'You remember Helen, don't you? We were at school together.'

'Of course, I remember her,' he snaps. 'She went to live in Athens soon after you left.' Then, with a shrug, he hands me my phone. 'I don't have much choice, do I? But you'll have to be quick.'

It only takes us a couple of minutes to get to the supermarket. I jump out of the car. He sits drumming his fingers on the steering wheel.

'Be quick, I shouldn't really park here.'

'Don't worry, I won't be long.' I know he won't get a ticket. He's just pissed off because he has to help me.

Grabbing a trolley, I throw cartons of milk, coffee, tea, pasta, sauce, pizza, salad stuff, nibbles and anything else we need on the trolley; then I remember the wine.

I take fifteen minutes and two trips to carry the bags and wine to the car. Nick's busy on his phone and ignores me. I shove it all in the back seat, then get in the front with him.

On the way back, he doesn't say much. I can tell he's nervous.

When we arrive back at the house, he sits tapping the steering wheel, waiting for me to get out.

'Come on Nick, I need some help; I'll take the shopping bags, you bring the wine.'

He rolls his eyes, grabs the wine and follows me inside, dumps it on the kitchen table and goes to leave. Then he suddenly stops. 'Oh, I nearly forgot, bring Helen to the ball tonight. I'll pick you up around 7ish.'

13

BETH & HELEN

OXFORD

I'VE JUST ABOUT FINISHED TIDYING up and washing my hair when there's a familiar knock on the door.

Helen looks at me anxiously as I open it. 'Oh Beth, I've been so worried about you.'

'I'm alright,' I laugh. 'Come here.'

I give her a hug, then haul her into the hall. 'You must be exhausted; let's go into the kitchen. It's the only decent room we have downstairs.'

Suddenly there's the familiar ping of a text coming through. My phone's still on the kitchen table where Nick left it.

Don't forget to tell Helen about tonight. I'll be there at 7.00.

I groan to myself, grab the phone, and delete the message. Helen's watching me, a look of surprise on her face.

'That was a text from Nick. You remember Nick from

school, don't you?'

She nods.

'Well, he just invited us to a charity ball - I'll text him back in a minute and say we're too tired.'

She looks puzzled. 'I didn't know you were such good friends. Isn't he that geeky little guy who used to follow you around?'

I look at her and frown. 'I don't remember that.'

'You must do. I think he had the hots for you.'

'Oh, be quiet.' I fill up the kettle and smile to myself. I won't tell her he's not so geeky anymore. Why bother? She'll soon find out.

She looks over towards the blackened door, then at me.

'I'll show it to you later, after you've had something to eat and a large glass of wine.'

She takes off her jacket, hangs it on the back of the kitchen chair, and looks around.

'So, where's Jamie?'

'He's staying with Mum for a few days.'

Helen looks surprised. 'But she's in Spain.'

I laugh. 'Yes, it's only for a few days till I get things sorted here. When I told Mum about the fire, she said she was getting the next flight back. I didn't want her to ruin her holiday, and we didn't want Jamie to stay here.'

'Your mum must be so worried.

I nod. 'Yes, that's why she suggested I call Nick.'

'But how can he help?'

'It turns out he's a detective inspector at the local police station; he knows all about my case.'

Now she looks surprised. 'Wow! I would never have thought he'd work for the police.'

I nod. 'Amazing, isn't it? Imagine how surprised I was when he invited us to this bloody charity ball tonight.'

'But I'd love to go.'

I make a face and switch on the kettle. 'It'll be a waste of time. Let's stay here. We can cook something nice, have a chat, drink some wine.'

'Come on Beth, you need to get out of here and Nick's such a sweetie.'

Maybe she's right. We have no TV, no comfortable chairs to sit on, just the kitchen table and a few hard chairs.

———

Helen's finishing getting ready when there's a knock on the door. Through the peephole, I can see Nick. He's wearing a tuxedo.

'Is that Nick?' she calls, running down the stairs.

'Shhh,' I say, pointing to the door.

She laughs and stands waiting for me to open it. She really looks stunning. Her long light brown hair is up in a French Pleat and my short black evening dress fits her like a glove.

'Shall I open the door?'

She nods.

Nick comes striding in. 'Helen, how lovely to see you! It's been so long since I saw you.'

She laughs and stands staring at him. 'It's lovely to see you, too. That tuxedo really suits you.'

He looks a bit embarrassed. 'You look great Helen, how are things in Athens?'

'Okay, how are things in Evesly?'

'Same as it's always been, nothing much changes around here.'

I stand observing them closely; I'm sure Helen blushed, and what a lovely smile Nick has.

He glances over at me and frowns. 'Are we ready?' I nod. 'Come on then, let's go.'

He turns and walks out of the house.

Helen turns to me, winks, and mouths. 'He's gorgeous!'

I laugh and follow them out, making sure to lock the door.

———

THE MAJOR'S HOUSE IS ONE of those lovely old Cotswold farmhouses oozing with charm. It's a pity I can't say the same about him. He barely looks at me, but I notice he manages a smile for Nick and Helen.

'I'm so glad you could come,' he croons in his smooth, upper-class voice. 'Please help yourselves at the buffet.'

Then he turns to Nick. 'You probably know everyone here. Be sure to introduce them to your friends.'

When saying this, he looks directly at Helen and ignores me.

Nick laughs and turns to Helen. 'I don't know what we'd do without him.' He prattles on about how wonderful the Major is and all the good deeds he does for the local community.

Just as I thought, it's going to be a long night. I look around for the ladies, then feel someone tugging at my arm.

It's Nick.

'Do you see what I mean, Beth?' He looks over at the Major and smiles. 'He's really quite nice once you get to know him.'

He leads me to a table, one of the round ones at the edge of the room. 'Now what would you like to drink, wine, champagne?'

'A glass of Sauvignon Blanc, if they have it.'

'Good, sit down; I'll be back in a minute.'

I sit on the edge of one of the claret-colored velvet chairs surveying the room. It's such a large room, and the way it's arranged, it looks more like a club than a living room. There's a buffet and bar at the far end, small tables scattered at the edge, and in the center is a small space for dancing.

Nick's talking to a couple of guys over at the buffet, the Major's introducing Helen to some of his cronies. I can tell by her face he has taken her in. He's cooing all over her and she's loving it.

Then the music starts. Out of the corner of my eye, I can see a tall guy with a huge beard heading towards me. I quickly get up, turn towards the bar and bump into Nick, holding our drinks.

'Careful,' he laughs. He places the drinks on a nearby table. 'Do you want to dance?'

Before I can answer the lights dim and the next thing I know, his arms are around me. There's a whiff of whisky on his breath, mingled with the French cologne he always seems to use.

He pulls me close; I gently push him away; he pulls me even closer.

We're like this for a couple of minutes until the music stops. Then he says he's going to the buffet and I'm left staring after him, wondering what that was all about.

Helen comes over, a wicked smile on her face. She nods in Nick's direction; I roll my eyes.

She laughs.

We head over to the buffet table, which is laden with tiny sandwiches stuffed with all kinds of things, such as salmon, beef, and cheese. Bowls of nuts, olives, and breadsticks. Two large roast turkeys on silver trays and two large fresh salmon decorated with caviar stand at each end of the table.

We find somewhere to sit, then Nick comes over and joins us. Helen gives me a wink and smiles at him sweetly; he asks her to dance. I sit watching them.

Is he going to pull her close, as he did with me?

But I don't have time to see what happens. Out of the corner of my eye, I see the guy with the beard walking towards me. I get up and go in search of the ladies.

It's such a large house and beautifully furnished. I wonder if the Major's married. I didn't see him with anyone tonight; maybe she's in London in their town house or apartment.

Half an hour later, it's finally over. It wasn't as bad as I thought it would be. At least we were out of the house for a while, and I stopped thinking about things.

On the way back, Helen sits in the front with Nick; I'm in the back. I thought he was coming onto me earlier tonight, but maybe he always dances like that.

The car skids to a halt. I jump out. Helen follows.

'Not inviting me in for coffee tonight, Beth?' he asks, poking his head out of the car window.

'Sorry Nick, but we're both tired. See you tomorrow.'

He grins and drives off.

'Dickhead,' I mutter, closing the front door.

Helen looks surprised. 'I thought he was very nice. Why do you say that?'

I shrug.

'You're too hard on him Beth, he was lovely tonight and so was the Major.'

I close the blinds. Maybe I am being grumpy, but I think I'm right about the Major.

14

BETH & HELEN

HELEN'S HOUSE
Evesly, The Cotswolds

'Good morning, Beth, working already?'

I look up, startled to see Helen up so early.

'Morning Helen, I was just looking for furniture for the living room. Mum and Jamie will be back soon so I must make a start on getting it ready for them.'

I was really looking for information on attacks in the area, but I don't tell her.

'Did you sleep well?'

'Like a log. I forgot how peaceful it is in Oxford.'

She sits in the chair opposite me, watching as I pour her a mug of steaming hot coffee.

'Here, you'll probably need this after last night. Sugars in the bowl if you need it.'

'Yes, I didn't realize how much I'd drunk. How do you feel?'

'Okay, I drank very little I have to be in the right mood and last night was a bit of a pain.'

Walking over to the window I look at the sun sparkling on the flowers and shrubs in the garden. 'What a lovely day. It's too nice to be cooped up in here. Where shall we go?'

I glance over at Helen; she's busy flicking through her phone.

'Helen, have some breakfast, then we can go for a drive, maybe have lunch by the river. What do you think?'

She quickly looks up. 'I'd love to, but I have to pop out for an hour. We can go out later when I come back.'

I place a plate of croissants in front of her.

'So, where are you going?'

'Oh, didn't I tell you? I'm meeting the estate agent at the house. It won't take me long; I'll be back soon.'

She breaks off a piece of croissant, chews it slowly, then washes it down with a gulp of coffee.

'But Mum's car is outside; I can drive you there.'

She shakes her head. 'It's best if you stay here, especially after what happened. I won't be long; we can go out later.'

'But Nick installed a tracking device on my phone; he can track wherever I go, didn't I tell you?'

She doesn't reply, just carries on chewing, which really pisses me off.

'Oh, come on Helen, it's a lovely day. Don't let that creep ruin it. He attacked me in the field behind your house, not in your house. Do you think he's watching me?'

She shrugs, which only makes me more irritated.

'Do you think he's going to follow me to your house?' I snort. 'The little shit's probably lying low or done a bunk. He knows I gave the police his description. It was in the local paper; if he shows his face around here, the police will catch him.'

Reluctantly, she agrees and goes to get ready.

———

The estate agent's car is outside when we arrive and she's busy talking on the phone.

Helen's been dreading this, and I can tell she wants to get it over with as quickly as possible.

Getting out of the car, I nod over to the agent. 'Let's go inside; I'll be in the garden if you need me.'

'Are you sure?' she asks, peering at me. 'You don't have to sit out there by yourself.'

I nod. 'Of course, I'll be alright; I'll check my emails, then give Mum a quick call.'

She gives me a hug. 'Okay, I won't be long. I'll be out in a minute.'

She disappears upstairs. I make my way down the narrow garden path. The scent of roses and honeysuckle fill the air. Weeds and small flowers poke their heads from every nook and cranny. It's a bit overgrown, but I love it.

We used to live just a five-minute walk from here. I wonder who lives there now? Mum and Dad rented it for a couple of years, then we went back to Athens.

At the far end of the garden, under a huge weeping willow tree, is the table we used to sit at most days to do our homework; it's slightly hidden from view and very shady.

I walk over and sit down. First, I'll call Mum and Jamie, then I'll check my emails.

As I go to take my phone from my shirt pocket, a large hand suddenly clamps over my mouth. I try to push it away, but I can't.

I'm being hauled over the low stone garden wall which surrounds the house. Then I'm on the ground. Someone's knees on my back, holding me down. Something's stuck over my mouth, then something's wrapped around my head. A van or car door creaks. I'm shoved inside. I fall to the floor; the door closes quietly.

I lay stunned for a few seconds. Then I remember the tracking device on my phone. Where is it?

With a jolt, the vehicle moves quickly away. I try to get a foothold but it's useless. I'm rolling around, then I feel something hard pressing against my breast. It's my phone then suddenly we stop. I try to get the thing off my head, but there's no time. The door opens and I'm hauled out.

Someone slaps me hard. I'm pulled along. Grass tickles my feet; my shoes must have fallen off.

A door creaks open. I'm pushed inside, my chest feels tight, I can hardly breathe.

'Go outside,' someone grunts. 'Check nobody's coming.'

A few seconds later, I hear the man come back.

'It's okay,' he mumbles. 'There's not a soul around. Get her over here.'

Their voices are eerie, they sound distorted. One of them touches me.

I'm hit and thrown face down over something hard, like a table. *If only I had my Glock I'm trained in Krav Maga but...*

One of them shouts, 'Get her pants down, quick.'

I can hardly breathe, the stuff over my mouth is choking me. I must focus, breathe through my nose, and try to keep calm.

They wrench off my trousers, then pull off my pants. I feel sick as they start groping me but I can't stop them. This goes on for some time their hands are all over me. Then one of them hisses, 'I'm going to fuck her move over.'

The other one says, 'No, I want to make her suffer. Get me that stick from over there.'

'Okay but let me have her first.'

'Get a move on then. Give her a good fuck, then let me have her.'

Zips are being pulled down; they're hold on me is not so tight anymore. It's the only chance I'll have. I must be quick.

I push back and turn, then with one almighty kick, I catch one of them in the balls. Someone yells. I keep kicking and kicking, trying to hit them.

'Fucking bitch, grab her. I'm going to kill her.'

Then there's a noise outside.

It's a car.

All goes quiet.

I hear the window open. They're getting away.

Someone shouts. 'Come out with your hands up. We know you're in there!'

I can't believe it; it's the police and the bastards are getting away.

The door crashes open. 'I'm Police Constable Felicity Bell. Shit!'

Something's thrown over me - probably a jacket.

'Keep still,' she mutters. 'Let me get this off your head.' She carefully removes the thing from my head and the tape from my mouth. 'Are you okay?' she asks.

A young PC with red hair is staring at me.

'Yes,' I mumble, whilst grabbing my pants from the floor. She passes me my trousers.

'We must get them,' I growl, pulling on my pants and pointing to the window. 'They escaped through there.' We run around the back, but nobody's there.

Suddenly I hear Nick shouting.

'Beth, are you alright?'

Followed

He comes running around the shed, then Helen appears.

She runs over and hugs me. 'Oh Beth, I'm so sorry. What happened?'

The sound of an engine starting up makes us swing round.

'Did you see a vehicle outside when you came?' I gasp. 'It was a car or a van, they used it to bring me here.'

Nick runs to his car. 'I'll get them, get in the car, hurry!'

But they are too far ahead. By the time the PC gets in the front and we get in the back, we've no chance of catching them. They've disappeared.

'Bastards, we should've got them!'

Helen's staring at me, her mouth's open. 'What happened, Beth?'

Nick's looking at me in the overhead mirror. 'Yes, what happened, Beth?'

PC Felicity Bell's talking on her phone, so he lowers his voice.

'I thought I told you to stay inside. It was just for a couple of days. Now, do you see why it was so important for me to add the tracker to your phone?'

Helen looks at Nick, then back at me. 'It's my fault. I should never have let you come with me today.'

'It's not your fault,' Nick groans. 'If Beth had stayed at home, none of this would have happened.'

I say nothing. What's the point? We sit in silence for a few minutes, then PC Felicity Bell tells Nick there's been an incident at the White Horse pub and to drop her there.

The PC gets out, Nick asks me to get in the front with him.

'What did they do to you?' he asks as soon as I get in and start buckling up.

So, I tell him. Helen gasps with shock. Nick looks angry.

'I'm taking you both back to my place, then we can decide what to do.'

'No, Nick, I want to go home.'

I can tell he's not happy, but he drives us to Mum's house.

When we arrive, Helen goes to make tea.

'Helen, I need something stronger than tea; there's some brandy over there, next to the bread bin. There's not much left, if you need another…'

She holds it up. 'There's enough for us all to have a drink.'

'Not for me, Helen, I'm driving.'

Helen nods, picks up two glasses from the draining board, then looks at Nick. 'Are you sure you don't want just a tiny one?'

'No, not now.'

Then he grabs me gently by the shoulders. 'Look Beth, it's no problem having you both stay for a while. I have plenty of room.'

I look at his worried face and shake my head. 'Nick, I told you before, I can take care of myself. They don't know who they're dealing with.'

I'm shaking with anger. I push past him, kick the kitchen door and stand glaring at it. 'When I get my hands on those bastards.'

'Are you out of your mind?' Nick yells, looking at me as if I'm crazy. 'You think you're so tough, but you don't know who you're dealing with.'

'And I suppose you do? I thought you didn't know who they were, Nick.'

His eyes nearly pop out of his head when I say this.

'Of course, I don't know who they are…' His voice trails off. It's as if he's struggling to control himself; then he turns and walks to the door. 'If you need me, you know where to find me.' He turns on his heel and leaves.

Through the window I can see him talking to the young police officer, then he gets in his car, winds down the window, and looks over at me.

'Remember what I said, Beth, don't go out.'

15

BETH & HELEN

OXFORD

HELEN HUGS ME. 'I don't know how you do it. If it were me, I'd...'

She shakes her head, squeezes my hand. 'You've been through a lot, Beth, but this has to stop.'

I know what she means but say nothing.

'Is there any more brandy or something strong?' she mutters, looking at the empty bottle of Metaxa brandy.

I point to one of the kitchen cupboards. 'There's more up there, on the right. Can you reach?'

She nods. 'I wish I didn't listen to you. I should've gone to the house by myself. It's the second time it's happened.'

She grabs a bottle of the 7-star Metaxa brandy we always bring back from Greece, unscrews the cap and starts topping up our glasses. 'You're in terrible danger next time you might not be so lucky.'

She hands me the brandy.

I gulp it down. 'Yes, I know what you mean. This time was different; they planned it and there were two of them.'

I sit staring into my glass trying to remember... it was something I read in the local paper; it was a terrible case which was headline news in Oxford.

Then I remember it was a gang of men who raped and abused young girls in the area for years yet nobody believed them, not even the police.

'Are you alright, Beth?' Helen asks, shaking me gently. 'Maybe you should see a doctor?'

'I'm fine, I was just thinking about something, nothing to do with this.' If Helen knew she'd shit herself with worry, so I won't tell her.

'Beth, promise me you'll leave it to the police. It's their job, they'll find them.' Then she grabs my hand. 'Shouldn't Nick have taken you to be examined, you know, in case they found... well, stuff for forensics?'

'It didn't get that far, Helen.'

'I just thought they might find something.' She goes to top up my glass again, I stop her.

'I need a shower and some fresh air. I can't stay in here.'

'But you can't, you heard what Nick said....'

'I don't care what he said, it will do us good to get out of this place.'

I race upstairs and stand under the shower, washing every trace of their filthy hands away.

I stand there for a long time, then rub myself dry, dress, then run downstairs.

'Are you ready, Helen?'

She sits staring at me.

There's a knock at the front door.

She rushes to open it.

In comes Nick.

I grab my jacket and head for the door. Nick stands in my way.

'Beth, I don't want you going anywhere.'

'Who asked you?' I growl, pushing past him.

He grabs my arm and shakes me. 'Calm down, the police are guarding the house, but if you go outside, how on earth can they protect you?'

I shake off his arm.

He grabs me again.

'What are you doing, Nick?'

He looks nervous and worried.

'Has this happened before, Nick? What aren't you telling me?'

He looks startled for a minute, then shakes his head. 'It's better if you don't know, these men are dangerous.'

So, I was right, he does know something.

'Tell me, Nick, I want to know.'

He says nothing, just stands looking at me, a strange look on his face.

Helen comes over and puts her arm around my shoulder. 'If you know something, Nick, you must tell her. She has a right to know.'

'Okay, if you must know, there have been a few attacks in the area, but we're onto them. If you stay inside, you'll be alright.'

I clench my fists, thinking about the girls I read about. They suffered so much for so many years and it's only recently the police finally believed them and put those guilty behind bars.

'Tell me about it, Nick, I need to know.'

His lips are set in a thin hard line, his eyes search my face. 'You said one of them was vicious. He wanted to…' His voice cracks, he swallows. 'The torture intended for you was used on this woman.'

I feel sick. Others are out there doing the same thing as those horrendous men who were recently jailed...

Helen has a look of horror on her face. Nick's pacing around the kitchen.

He swings round and looks at me. 'Do you still want to go out, Beth?'

I nod. 'I can't stay in here. I don't feel safe; we'd be better off in a hotel.'

He looks at Helen, then at me. 'Right, get a few things together; I'm taking you back to my house; there's plenty of room.'

I start to say something, but he cuts me off. 'Beth, you'll both be safe with me. It will give us time to sort something out.'

Before I can say anything, Helen's running upstairs. 'I'll get some things together for us.' She stops and looks at me. 'We can't stay here.'

Nick opens the back door, pulls out his phone and talks to someone.

A few minutes later, we're in his car.

'Don't worry, I've arranged for two armed officers to be outside my house. You'll be perfectly safe.'

He's driving fast down the country lanes—he's going faster and faster. I hang on tight. Every time we go around a bend, Nick's thigh presses against mine.

'Slow down, Nick,' Helen shouts from the back seat.

He slams on the brakes. 'Sorry.'

He's driving much slower now; he's taking the long way round to his house, probably to avoid going near Helen's place.

Suddenly, he drives fast again. What's wrong with him? Then he slows down and pulls up outside a large house.

'This is it; stay here. I won't be a minute.'

He slides out of the car and hurries over to where two armed police officers are standing. He talks to them, then beckons to us to go inside.

I don't know what I was expecting, but it wasn't this.

Snow white carpets, an expensive-looking chandelier towering above us, and the living room - well, it's huge, with large French windows leading into a garden.

Two long red sofas and four deep, comfortable looking armchairs set around a large open fireplace. It's lovely.

He switches on a couple of table lights that give a cozy feel, then gestures for us to sit down. 'Make yourselves at home. Drinks are over there in the cabinet; I'll be back in a minute.'

I can feel Helen watching me. 'I'm booking you a ticket,' she says, leaning over and giving me a reassuring hug. 'You're coming back to Athens with me for a while.'

16

NICK'S HOUSE

A LITTLE LATER NICK RETURNS, he walks over to the drinks cabinet, which is well stocked with bottles of wine, champagne, beer and soft drinks.

'What can I get you?'

Helen smiles. 'White wine for me, please.'

'And you, Beth?'

'Sauvignon Blanc if you have it.'

He nods, flicks through the bottles, then chooses one. 'I'm heating some food; it won't take long, and yes Beth, it is veggie.'

He hands us our drinks. 'Tell me what you think of the wine.'

I sit, swilling the wine around in the glass, then take a sip. It's really very good. I can see him watching me and smile. 'It's one of the best I've tasted, Nick.'

I can tell that's pleased him. His face softens. He looks happy for a change. He's a weird guy. Sometimes I really like him, other times he makes me nervous, he's very intense, maybe if he relaxed a little?

He turns and takes out a beer. 'I'll make up some beds in a minute, then you can get some rest.'

'Don't worry, Nick, we can make the beds later.' I'm not hungry either, but I don't say that. Under normal circumstances, I might enjoy this, but I'm on edge. I can't stop thinking about those men and what they did to me. I sip my wine; Helen talks about when they were at school.

'You used to live with your parents in the village, Nick, didn't you?'

He laughs. 'That was a long time ago; they live up North now. I was married for a while, then after the divorce I sold the house and came here; the other house was too large for just me.'

Now he has surprised me; houses in the Cotswold don't come cheap; if this is smaller than his first house, the other house must have cost him a fortune.

Helen goes with Nick into the kitchen to get the food.

I'm curious to see what the kitchen's like and just like the rest of the house — it's amazing. The kitchen's enormous with granite work surfaces and the latest high-end equipment.

The microwave pings, Nick grabs some bowls and begins scooping piping hot lasagna into them. I usually love the stuff, but not now. The thought of eating makes me want to puke.

I turn and walk back into the living room. 'I'm not hungry Nick, maybe later.'

He follows with the bowls of food. 'You won't offend me if you leave it. Just try to eat something; it will do you good.'

I try, but I can't swallow. I keep shoving bits of pasta

around the plate with my fork, pretending I'm eating. Then, to my relief, Nick's phone rings.

'Sorry, I have to take this. I'll be back in a minute.'

Helen stacks up the bowls with my leftover lasagna on top and carries them into the kitchen. I'm told to stay in the living room and rest, she'll wash the dishes.

I sit thinking about what Nick said. This has happened before, so...

Suddenly the water's turned off, the sound of washing up coming from the kitchen dies down. I can hear Helen talking quietly to Nick; I try to catch what they're saying, but the door's closed.

A couple of minutes later, Nick comes in with a tray of coffee and chocolate biscuits and plonks them on the table.

Helen sits on the sofa opposite me and starts flicking through her iPad. Nick sits next to her.

'There's a flight leaving at 11.30 am, tomorrow with Aegean Airways,' she says, peering at me over her iPad.

What does she want me to say? She knows I'm not going; I lean forward and take the coffee Nick hands me.

He gives me one of his serious looks and stands looking at me with his soft brown eyes. 'She's right, go back with Helen. Your mum and Jamie can join you later.'

I groan and roll my eyes. 'Not this again. How many times do I have to tell you?'

Nick leaps to his feet and stands staring at me. 'And what exactly are you going to do here, Beth?'

'I'm going to find the bastards who did this.'

He turns and looks out of the window, then swings round and glares at me. 'Why are you being so stubborn? Think of your son; he needs a mother, not a corpse.'

I can't believe he just said that. 'That's why I'm not going to Athens. I'm thinking of them; these monsters must be stopped. If you lot got your act together...'

His face is ashen, I can tell he's trying to control himself; he looks over to Helen for support; she just rolls her eyes and looks away. He comes over and squats down in front of me.

'Okay, stay here with me at least then I'll know you're safe.'

'No Nick, I can't stay here. I'm staying at Mum's and if you don't like it...'

He grabs my hands. 'What do I have to do? I'm only trying to help. If you won't stay here, I'll come and stay with you.'

Shit. I didn't think of that.

Then a thought comes to me. This could work to my advantage.

Helen sighs, puts down her iPad and sits next to me. 'Beth, you know what I think, but it's up to you.'

I sit, thinking of what Nick said. If he stays with me, he can have Jamie's room, it's not very large, but there's a double bed and most of the time he'll be at work, he won't be any trouble, and it won't be for long, just a couple of days at the most.

'Okay, but if you stay with me, Nick, you must let me help. I want them caught.'

He's looking at me with a weird smile on his face; sometimes I wonder what he's really thinking.

'Okay. I'll pack a few things and leave them at your place when I drop you off in the morning.'

When he's gone, Helen turns to me. 'Beth, I have four bedrooms; there's enough room for all of us. Jamie can go back to his old school. You know your mum loves Athens, so do you.'

'Helen, I would love to, but that won't solve anything, will it?'

'I think it will. At least you'll be safe. I don't want to leave you here, for God's sake Beth, it's not safe.'

'Don't worry Helen, I'll be alright, I have the police guarding me and Nick.'

'Yes, but for how long?'

At that moment, Nick comes back into the room; he gives me a strange look.

'It's getting late; why don't we all go to bed? We can talk about this again in the morning.'

I look at him in surprise. 'But Nick, we just decided that you were going to stay with me.'

He shrugs. 'I just thought it would give us time to think. Anyway, if you need anything, give me a shout. I'm a light sleeper.'

'I don't have to think about anything my mind's made up.'

He sighs, shrugs his shoulders as if to say, *you win,* then goes to bed.

Half an hour later, after dozing on the couch, Helen and I go to our room.

'Wow, this is nice,' Helen murmurs, touching the white, pristine duvet on one of the beds. 'As well as being good looking, he has good taste.'

I grunt. 'I noticed you two are getting on well together, maybe...'

She laughs. 'He has eyes for only you, Beth. Surely you can see that.'

Ignoring her, I slip off my jeans and snuggle under the crisp white duvet. 'Wow, it's so comfortable. What do you think, Helen?'

'Let's say it won't take me long to sleep tonight. Night, Beth.'

Helen soon falls asleep, and even though I'm shattered, sleep evades me. I lay thinking of what happened, then shiver, remembering what they did and feel icy cold all over. With Nick's help, we need to catch them.

I'm just dropping off when I'm sure I heard a car pull up outside.

I lay there trying to listen.

Shall I get up and peek out of the window to see who it is?

But I'm so tired, my eyes keep closing...

17

NICK'S HOUSE

The following morning...

It seems strange waking up in Nick's house. Helen's still asleep, so I crawl out of bed, creep over to the window and peer out.

Our bedroom's in the house's front. I can see the two police officers who were there last night, then I remember the car I heard. I wonder who it was?

Tiptoeing to the en-suite bathroom so as not to disturb Helen, I have a quick shower. Everything in this house is top-notch. The beds, the bathroom, even the tiny chocolates Nick placed on the pillows last night were a nice touch.

'Is that you, Beth?' Helen calls from the bedroom.

'Yes, I'm just having a quick shower. We don't have long. Nick's dropping us off first, then he's going to work.'

I wrap the soft white bathrobe around me and pad into our bedroom, enjoying the luxury of the deep piled carpet.

Helen crawls out of bed, staggers over to the bathroom, rubbing her eyes. 'I couldn't keep my eyes open last night. It must have been all that brandy and wine. Now I'm dying for a coffee.'

'I'll get dressed quickly, go downstairs and see if Nick's around.'

A couple of minutes later, I'm downstairs, heading for the kitchen.

Nick looks up as I open the door. He's drinking coffee and looks just like he always does; I don't know how he does it. I on the other hand, feel like crap and probably look it.

'Did you sleep well?' he asks, sipping his coffee.

'Yes, the bed was very comfortable.'

He smiles, puts down his cup and pours me a coffee. 'There's juice in the fridge and toast keeping warm under the grill. I'm just going to put my things in the car, so be quick. We must get going soon.'

After breakfast, Nick drops us off at Mum's, then drives to work.

———

Back at Mum's place Helen switches on the kettle, then we go into the garden.

Helen sighs and starts walking around the garden. 'Well, at least we've got the garden. It could be worse.'

I remember saying those same words to Jamie when we came back from the hospital; it seems so long ago, but it's only a couple of days.

'I'll get Nick's room ready,' I call, going back inside. 'I'll also give Mum a quick call.'

'Do you want something to eat?' she asks, following me in from the garden.

'No, but I'd love a coffee.'

Once I've changed the bed linen, I leave the window slightly ajar for fresh air, then call Mum.

As soon as she answers I can tell something's wrong. 'What is it Mum? Is Jamie okay? Are you alright?'

She seems hesitant at first, but then it all comes spilling out. 'Oh Beth, I didn't want to worry you, but I think I must. Jamie's not very happy. He's trying to put on a brave face, but he's worried about school; he doesn't want to go back to Oxford, he wants to go to Athens with you.'

'Mum, he hasn't really given it a chance, has he? He's only been there a couple of days.'

'But he misses his friends and the life he had in Athens.'

'I discussed it with him,' I reply sharply. 'He thought it would be great; he couldn't wait to get on the plane. I know he's not really fitting in, but he must give it a chance once he makes friends he'll be alright. Anyway, all the schools are full, you should know; don't you remember how difficult it was to get him in here?'

'Yes, I know, but he really hates the school.'

'Mum, please don't worry, I'll talk to Jamie. We'll sort something out.'

I don't know what, but what else can I say?

'Oh, I nearly forgot, Helen's here. She's staying for a few days, then going back to Athens.' I know this will make her happy and it does; I can hear the relief in her voice.

'That's good. I've been so worried thinking about you all by yourself, call me if you need anything, okay? Now I'll pass you to Jamie; he wants to talk to you.'

'Mum, when are you coming to Spain? I thought you'd be here by now.'

'Soon, I'm just trying to sort things out here. How are you? What have you been doing?'

'You know I'm not going back to that school, don't you, Mum?'

I'm shocked by the desperation in his voice. 'Don't worry, I'll sort something out.'

He says nothing and hands me back to Mum. I can hear her telling him to get a drink for her from the fridge.

'You see Beth,' she whispers. 'He's really worried. Maybe you should go back to Athens.'

I'm just about to say something when she changes the subject.

'Oh, I forgot, I've transferred some money to your account, buy some new furniture, I'm not waiting for the insurance to pay up — we need it now.'

'Okay Mum, any particular style or colour?'

'You choose; now take care, I'll call you tomorrow, and say hello to Helen for me.'

I hurry downstairs to the garden. 'Helen, Mum said to say hello.' I stop when I see her; she's peering at her iPad with such a worried look on her face.

She smiles. 'That's nice, I hope they're enjoying themselves in Spain.' Then she points to the coffee. 'Have some while it's hot. Are you sure you're not hungry?'

'I had a piece of toast at Nicks.'

She sits staring at her iPad. 'Beth, I've been thinking, I know you want to stay here but if you come back with me, just for a few days, it will give you a chance to think more clearly.'

Here we go. 'Helen, I know you're trying to help, but you know I have to stay here; Nick says they're doing all they can, but I'm not so sure.'

She gives me a reproachful look. 'So, ask him to get more people on the case?'

She's right. Then I think of that awful place they took

me to. What if they take more women there? Nick says it's a crime scene now, but who's to stop them? The police aren't there all the time.

'Just a minute Helen, I must call Nick.'

Maybe there's CCTV inside the shed?

I quickly tap in his number, but it goes to voicemail, so I leave a message:

This is urgent, call me back quickly.
   Beth

18

OXFORD
Late morning...

NICK STILL HASN'T CALLED me back and Helen's busy on her iPad.

I try calling him again; it goes to voicemail.

I pace around the garden. 'Where can he be?'

Helen frowns. 'Beth, you know I can't stay here any longer, Tula has another job. She's only filling in for me to make some extra cash. I'm booking a flight for tomorrow morning. I can get tickets for your mum and Jamie to come to Athens; it will be like old times. Imagine how happy Jamie will be.'

I knew she'd try to make me go back with her, but this is getting ridiculous.

'Helen, we both know I have to stay, so let's not discuss it anymore, please.'

She shrugs, goes back to looking at her iPad. I pick up the empty cups and go inside.

I start washing up then suddenly feel bad. She's only trying to help. I'd probably do the same if this was happening to her. Leaning forward over the sink, I open the window.

'I know, let's go to the pub, we can have an early lunch?'

She looks up, closes her iPad and comes inside. 'Beth, you know we can't, anyway we don't need to look at all the food there is in the fridge.'

'I feel like a caged animal. I can't stay in here all the time.'

She laughs. 'I know, so come back to Athens with me.'

I roll my eyes; will she never stop?

'Okay, but if you want to stay here, promise me you'll stay inside, and if you have to go out, take Nick with you.' She suddenly looks very serious. 'You realise it might take weeks to catch them? What will you do when your mum comes back?'

I look at her in desperation. Hasn't she been listening to me? 'That's why I'm so worried, Helen. Mum and Jamie can't come back here with those nutters on the loose. The police won't keep the officers guarding us here for much longer. They can't afford it. I think Nick's behind them being here.'

I pace around the garden. 'It's very good of him and all that, but for how long can they do it? What happens when they leave? What if Mum and Jamie come back and those evil bastards are still on the loose?'

Helen sits staring at her iPad. 'I'm so worried about you. You've been through so much, what with Athens and now this.'

'What happened in Athens seems a lifetime ago, but you're right.' I shrug. 'Why the hell does everything go wrong?'

She comes over and hugs me. 'I just can't bear to think of you being here all by yourself.'

I look at her sad face; she came all the way to see me. I feel so angry, so frustrated. *Why haven't the police caught them?*

'Are you alright, Beth?'

'Of course, I was just thinking.' I force myself to smile. 'I know. Let's make something nice to eat or shall I order something online?'

She opens the fridge. 'With all this vegan and veggie cheese we can make macaroni cheese; it's quick and easy. You used to love it.'

'I still do; I love home-made food, but recently I haven't felt much like cooking.'

'I know. I often eat salads and ready-made meals. It's not worth cooking just for one, is it?'

I look at her in surprise. 'But you're not on your own. What about *your* Theo? He loves his home-cooked meals?'

She pulls a face, mumbles something about him always working and changes the subject.

———

AFTER EATING, Helen calls Tula about her flight - I leave her to it, go into the garden and start flicking through my phone.

A few minutes later, there's a knock on the door. It's Nick. He sniffs the air and gives me a huge grin. 'Something smells good, Beth.'

He follows me into the kitchen, opens the oven door and peers inside. 'Wow! I didn't know you could cook.'

I laugh. 'Well, hurry and get changed before it gets cold.'

He disappears upstairs to get out of his work clothes. I go back into the garden.

About fifteen minutes later, after he's changed and eaten, he joins me in the garden. Helen's gone to the bathroom.

'Thanks Beth, it makes a change to have home-made food; it was delicious.'

I laugh. He gives me one of his funny looks and plonks his laptop down beside me.

I move up to give him some room and glance at him sideways. He's changed into lighter clothes, there's a hint of the French cologne he always uses; suddenly I realise how good looking he is.

I'm still watching him as he taps in his password, and without meaning to, I see what it is. It's quite simple and wouldn't be difficult to hack. He seems oblivious, so I take a quick sip of wine and look away.

Helen comes into the garden with a smile on her face.

I give her a frown. 'I'll get another bottle,' I mumble, jumping up. 'Be back in a minute.'

As soon as I'm in the kitchen, I jot down his password on the back of Mum's calendar. You never know, I might need it.

Back in the garden, Helen gives me one of her knowing smiles. I just ignore her and tell them about the new furniture I ordered.

'Mum asked me to choose the colour. I hope it's alright, it's being delivered tomorrow.' Then I remember the state of the living room. 'Oh no, the room! I'll have to clear it out.'

'Great,' Nick mutters, not looking up from his laptop. 'Where are you going to put all the rubbish?'

'Don't worry, we'll help,' chimes in Helen, laughing. 'I

need a bit of exercise. We'll need black rubbish bags and a couple of strong brushes.'

Nick groans, puts down his laptop. 'I'll change into my old clothes. Be back in a minute.'

With the three of us doing it, we're soon finished. Nick takes the rubbish bags out while I get the drinks and nibbles ready.

'When's your flight, Helen?' Nick asks, coming back into the kitchen to wash his hands.

'It's at 9.30 tomorrow morning, from Luton Airport.' Then under her breath, she mutters. 'I just wish Beth was coming with me.'

Nick starts sipping his wine, but I can see him watching me out of the corner of his eye.

'Fancy an early morning drive, Nick? The roads won't be busy if we leave early. It'll only take an hour if we hurry.'

He shakes his head. 'I would if I could, but I've a lot on tomorrow.'

Helen stands up. 'I'll take the train back to the airport; it doesn't take long, so please don't worry, Beth.'

'Okay, then I'm booking you a taxi.'

Nick looks over at Helen. 'Don't worry. I'll look after her when you're gone.'

19

OXFORD
Early Morning

'Taxi's here. Hurry!' Nick shouts, opening the front door.

Helen wraps her arms around me and hugs me as if she'll never see me again. 'Take care and call me.'

One last wave and she's gone.

Nick says something to the young police officer in the garden, then gets into his car and winds down the window.

'If you're worried about anything, let the officer know or call me - okay?'

I nod.

He gives a mock salute and drives off.

I feel restless; Helen's on her way to Athens, Nick's gone to work, and I'm stuck here. I watch his car until it turns the corner, then go inside.

On the kitchen table sit the remnants of breakfast. Helen's half eaten croissant and Nick's empty plate. He had two slices of toast with beans on top, and two more on the side, one of which he left.

I sit absentmindedly, spreading Vegemite over the leftover slice, when suddenly my foot touches something hard. I take a quick look under the table and see Nick's laptop; he must have forgotten it.

Wiping the crumbs of toast from my hands, I reach down and haul it up onto the table. I sit looking at it for a few minutes.

This is his work laptop, so everything relating to these awful rape and assault cases could be right here. He doesn't have a key, so he'll have to knock to come in.

I remember his password so quickly login.

I take a while to find what I'm looking for, but when I do, I'm stunned. Some details are missing, such as where it happened, but there's a lot to go on, much more than I expected.

A slight tap at the door makes me swing round. Shit, he's back. I quickly log out, shove the laptop back under the table, and stand up.

There's another tap at the door.

I run to the living room and peer through the blinds; it's a delivery man. It's the furniture I ordered.

Ten minutes later I'm surveying a new red sofa and two large red chairs, the plastic covering will have to stay until we've decorated the room, we also need new flooring, or a carpet fitted, but for now this will have to do.

Then I remember Nick's laptop. Mum has a printer in her bedroom.

With his laptop under my arm, I run upstairs.

Fifteen minutes later, Nick's laptop is back under the kitchen table, and I'm upstairs going through my printouts.

All the women who reported being raped or assaulted

and subsequently retracted their statements, I highlight in green. There aren't many, but I must investigate them.

The notes made by Nick; I circle in red, then I jot down a couple of the victim's names and addresses and phone numbers. I'll call them later.

Now what am I going to say to them? Will they talk to me? These are all things I must prepare for.

What would I say if someone called me—would I put down the phone?

I must tell them who I am first and why I want to talk to them, then see them as soon as possible.

I scribble a few ideas down, then I put the printer away, hide the printouts in Mum's wardrobe and glance out of the window.

It's such a lovely day; I'd love to go for a walk to clear my head, but the police officer downstairs has strict instructions to monitor me. If I leave the house, he'll call Nick.

Just as I'm about to move away from the window a white van catches my eye. Someone's in the driver's seat—I can't see them clearly. I look for a little longer. It's just a van—it could belong to anyone. Am I'm getting paranoid?

20

OXFORD
Late afternoon...

A SPANAKOPITA (feta cheese and spinach pie) and a tray of fat red peppers, stuffed with rice and herbs, are cooking in the oven. I'm curled up on one of the new chairs in the living room, a large glass of white wine in my hand.

After dinner, I'll tell Nick what I intend to do; I have no choice. Hopefully, he'll help, but whatever happens, I must meet at least one of the women I found on his laptop.

My phone rings. It's Nick.

'Sorry I'm late. I'll be there in a few minutes. Do we need anything for dinner?

'No, I've cooked; it'll be ready soon, so hurry.'

Ten minutes later, he's in the kitchen.

He squats down in front of the oven and peers inside.

'I could get used to this,' he says, sniffing the food.

'Scrumptious looking pie, stuffed peppers and all homemade.'

He stands up, gives me a sort of hug, then disappears upstairs. 'I'll get changed, be down in a minute.'

I know his few minutes; he'll probably have a shower and I'm hungry so I go to the bottom of the stairs and call up to him.

'I'm going to eat, then I'll be in the garden; you can serve yourself.'

No reply, he must be having a shower.

Fifteen minutes later, he comes out and joins me with a plateful of food. Scooping up a forkful of pie, he pops it into his mouth. 'This is delicious Beth; you should be a cook.'

I sit, sipping my wine thoughtfully while he cleans his plate, glad he's enjoying it. I don't really know much about him. He never talks about his ex-wife or says anything about a girlfriend.

'When you were married, did your wife do all the cooking?

Why the hell did I say that? What do I care if she did or not? Alex and I started out doing everything together, but that didn't last long.

'I wasn't there much,' he says, wiping his mouth on a piece of kitchen roll, then he glugs down some beer and carries on eating. 'I ate at work most of the time and at weekends we'd get a take-away or she cooked.' He pauses, as if remembering, then smiles. 'It was all so quick - I asked her out and a month later we were married.'

He's surprised me now. 'So, it was an on the spur sort of thing?'

'Yes, I suppose you could say that. At first, we were happy, then I changed jobs. Viv, that's my wife, well she was often alone. I thought she was okay; I was making good money.' He looks thoughtful for a minute, then gives a shrug. 'We had a lovely house. Then one day she just upped and left.'

'That's awful, Nick, I'm so sorry.'

He nods in agreement. 'Yes, and a few days later she calls and leaves a message asking for a divorce.' He shrugs and finishes his food. 'What about you?'

'Oh, it was just one of those things,' I mumble. Only Helen and Mum and a few good friends know about it. I don't feel comfortable telling Nick, although I like him a lot, I don't really know him.

'What happened?' he asks, leaning forward, an unlit cigarette in his hand.

'Oh, it's a long story.'

He sits drinking his beer, watching me. 'Did Helen know? Was she in Athens with you?'

'Yes, but she was having problems with her travel agency; she's lucky James was there. Do you remember him? He was in our class at school in Evesly.'

He nods. 'Yes, he moved to Athens also, didn't he?'

I'm amazed he remembers I didn't think he knew James that well.

'Yes, he's a good friend Helen and him are very close.'

He looks surprised. 'I thought she was married?'

I laugh. He knows everything, doesn't he?

'Yes, she is.'

I stand up and stretch, then catch Nick watching me; he looks away and lights his cigarette.

'Nick, we must do something. This has gone on for far too long—it's not safe here and Mum will be back soon.'

He nods in agreement. 'You're right, so what do you suggest?'

'I've been doing some research; I know how we can catch them.'

His eyes nearly pop out of his head; he sits staring at me for a long time then sighs. 'You must leave this to me, Beth. You're already a target, you'll only inflame the situation.' He raises an eyebrow and looks at me strangely. 'And we don't want that, do we?'

I knew it wouldn't be easy, but this is ridiculous; what the hell's wrong with him?

'Nick, I've got to do something; if I leave it to the police, nothing's going to get done, is it?'

He sits looking at me for a moment, stubs out his cigarette and stands up.

'For God's sake Nick, sit down.'

His eyebrows shoot up.

'Look, I'm only trying to help—I've been researching cases of rape and assault in Evesly and the Oxford area.'

He sits down and stares at me.

'Nick, the people who commit these crimes are just plain evil; they enjoy hurting people.'

A muscle twitches in his cheek; his lips press together in a thin tight line.

'You do nothing, okay?'

His voice is so cold, I feel a shiver run down my spine.

What's wrong with him?

I glare at him. 'No, I won't do nothing Nick; have you ever wondered why victims of rape don't confide in the police?'

I lean forward and lower my voice. 'These cases should be solved by now, but they're not, are they?'

Before he can say anything, I carry on. 'The women need someone to confide in. They need someone like me —

someone they can relate to — someone who understands what they've gone through.'

He suddenly grabs my face with both hands. It's as if he's going to kiss me; then he laughs. 'You may be right, Beth, but that's never going to happen.' He's looking at me with a strange expression on his face, then he lets go of my face and picks up his beer.

'Nick, I'll phone a couple of the victims and arrange to see them; I'll go by myself, or you can take me.'

He raises his eyebrows and shakes his head. 'You're stark raving mad!' Then his eyes narrow. 'And how do you know their names and phone numbers?'

Shit. Now what do I say?

'How do you think? I went on-line, found some articles, the rest was easy, I'm not an investigative journalist for nothing. Come on Nick, it won't take long. I'll arrange to meet one of them tomorrow in the afternoon, okay?'

He sits shaking his head. 'And if I don't help?'

'Need you ask?'

He stands up as if to go. I jump up and stand in front of him.

'I'll disguise myself, even you won't recognise me.'

He's watching me closely; his eyes are like slits, he looks different, and then he smiles. 'Okay, show me.'

I run upstairs and ten minutes later I'm back in the kitchen wearing a black wig and one of Mum's old three-quarter length dresses. Fortunately, we're the same size, so the dress fits.

I walk over and give him a twirl. 'What do you think?'

He leans forward and laughs. 'You don't look any different.'

'Well, that's because you know it's me. Get me a police

uniform, I'll pull down the cap, then you won't recognise me.'

He's looking at me in that strange way again, then gets up. 'I'll talk to you in the morning. I'm going to bed—I have an early start.'

I watch him go. It feels strange, just the two of us here.

'Night,' I call after him. How strange, I'm getting used to having him here. The dimly lit kitchen that had just seemed so cozy now feels creepy. The light from the hallway casts shadows on the wall and I shiver. I peer through the kitchen window and gasp. It's only the officer, but he made me jump.

I suddenly hear Nick's bedroom door close. He must've finished in the bathroom, so I turn off the lights and head upstairs to my room and sit, wondering what Mum would think if she knew Nick was here.

Shall I call Mum? It's nearly 11pm so midnight in Spain, she's probably asleep.

After brushing my teeth, I slip into a nighty, snuggle under the duvet, leaving the bedside light on. Just to make sure, I reach under my pillow and feel the handle of the kitchen knife. I close my eyes, but sleep evades me.

I lay in bed listening to the sounds of the night, an owl calling to its mate, the sound of a passing car... I wonder if Nick's asleep.

Then I freeze.

What was that?

There it goes again; it's coming from outside.

I reach for my knife, slide out of bed, and creep onto the landing.

'What the hell are you doing out here?' It's Nick. Then he notices the knife in my hand. 'Are you crazy?' he hisses. 'Go back to your room!'

He goes downstairs; I follow.

Suddenly there's a crash. The front door swings open. Standing in the doorway, wearing a balaclava, is a man holding a gun.

With one hand, Nick pushes me behind him, then someone shouts.

'Police, put your hands up.'

The man swears, then turns and runs.

Nick's face is like a mask in the moonlight; then he turns and looks at me, 'Stay inside.'

I don't move.

'Do you want to get killed?' he hisses, grabbing me and shoving me inside the house.

He turns and runs down the garden path with the other police officer. I follow him but trip over something. It's the young police officer from the front garden—he's covered in blood.

I bend down to feel for his pulse. Shit!

Running back inside to the kitchen, I grab the house phone and dial 999.

'I need an ambulance, someone's been hurt. Come quick, I can't feel his pulse.'

21

BETH VISITS JANE

The following day...

I'M in the kitchen thinking about the CCTV the police installed over the front of the house a few days ago. The guy who broke in last night was wearing a balaclava, so even with CCTV, we didn't know who he was.

It's supposed to be installed along the street, but so far nothing's been done. I must remind Nick to talk to them about it. Maybe the hooded guy came in a car, or someone dropped him off. If we had CCTV in the street, the police would have something to go on.

'I'm late,' Nick yells, hurtling down the stairs into the kitchen. 'Where's my laptop?'

I smile to myself. 'It's probably under the table where you left it. You don't have to rush, it's only ten past eight.' I pass him a plate of freshly made bacon sandwiches.

His eyes widen. 'Bacon sandwiches?'

'Yeah.'

He takes a bite and grimaces. 'What sort of bacon is this? It tastes like wood.'

He looks so funny; I can't help but laugh. 'Here, put some HP sauce on it.'

'No, it's okay.' He rams the rest into his mouth, then takes a sip of coffee. 'Don't you miss eating real bacon?'

'No, I prefer this.'

He raises an eyebrow, takes another large gulp of coffee, and turns to go.

'What about the young PC? Is there any news?'

'He's critical, but they think he'll pull through. Now I must go, or I'll be late.'

'Don't forget to chase them up on putting CCTV in our street; if it was there last night, we might have caught him getting out of a car or something.'

He grunts.

'Nick, I'll try to see one of the women today. What time shall I make it?'

He frowns and looks irritated.

'Come on Nick, last night you said you would take me.'

'I said nothing of the sort,' he declares, feigning surprise. Then he gives me one of his serious looks. 'You know I could get into trouble for this, don't you?'

I hadn't thought of that.

He stares at me for a long time, as if deciding what to do.

I turn and walk over to the window. He follows.

Placing his hands on my shoulders, he says quietly, 'I'll be busy most of the day, but if it must be today, make it around 12.30 lunchtime, then call and let me know.'

I watch him drive away, then bolt the door, run upstairs and take out my notes.

The first woman I call cuts me off after just a few seconds. The next one seems hesitant, but I keep talking. I explain what happened to me, and why I'm calling. 'Did you have a similar experience?' I ask, holding my breath.

Silence.

I don't want to frighten her, so I lower my voice. 'I want to help you. I want to catch the people who did this. We must talk. Can we meet somewhere?'

'Who are you?' she demands. 'Are you with the police?'

I glance at my notes. Her name is Jane Furrows.

'Jane, I'm a friend of Detective Inspector Nick Stephens; you can phone him if you like, he'll confirm it. I live in Oxford with my mother and son.'

Silence.

'Jane! Are you still there?'

'Yes.'

'Now listen carefully, Jane, do you have a pen? Good! Now take down my name and phone number.'

I give her time to jot it down.

'Can we meet today, Jane? Maybe lunch time, around 12.30?'

She hesitates for a minute. 'At my house?'

'Yes, if you want to. Do you live at the same address you gave the police last year?'

'Yes.'

I read it out to her, just to make sure it's the correct address. It is. 'Okay Jane, I'll see you soon.'

'Wait, how will I know it's you?'

I'm just about to say I'm 5'4' with blonde hair, then remember I'll be in disguise.

'I have long black hair and I'm of medium height. DI Stephens will drop me off in his black VW Golf; he'll wait outside, so there's nothing to worry about.'

We say goodbye; I sit staring at my phone for a few minutes, then I call Nick.

Although he tries to brush me off saying he's too busy and that he has a meeting to go to, he eventually agrees to collect me around 12.00 mid-day.

For the next few hours, I pace around the bedroom rehearsing what I'm going to say, then I get dressed.

At 12.10, my phone rings; it's Nick, he's outside.

Checking my notepad and phone are in my bag, I leave. Out of the corner of my eye, I can see the new police officer watching me as I walk around the corner to Nick's car.

We drive to Jane's house in silence. He parks a little further down the street from where her house is. He looks anxious but says nothing.

I open the door, then turn to look at him. 'Don't worry, I won't be long.'

He just nods and watches me walk to her house.

I ring the doorbell. No answer: I press my finger on it harder. This time, I hear someone coming.

A young woman with long red curly hair and large blue eyes opens the door.

'Jane? It's me, Beth.'

Her eyes search behind me to see if anyone's watching, then, as if satisfied, she beckons me inside.

I follow her into the living room where a large fluffy black cat reclines on a sofa. Raising its head, it looks at me suspiciously.

'What a lovely cat. Is he yours?'

'Yes, and she's a girl.'

She motions to a chair for me to sit down.

The cat doesn't take her eyes off me. 'Do you live here alone?' I ask, eyeing the cat.

'No, it's my parent's house.'

I can tell she's nervous—she wants to get it over with quickly, and so do I.

'Jane, I have to record this.' I take out my phone and place it on the table in front of us. 'Is that alright?'

She frowns and looks confused.

'We have to do this. It might happen again and next time you might not get away and...'

A look of horror crosses her face, she nods, I press record.

'It was so terrible.' Her voice is so soft I can hardly hear it. I mouth *louder* and she nods. The cat snuggles close to her as if to comfort her. I just sit and hold my breath.

'Where did it happen?' I ask, trying to keep my voice steady.

No reply.

'Where did it happen, Jane?'

She says nothing.

'Was it a car? Did they pick you up and drive you somewhere?'

Still, she says nothing, so in desperation I ask. 'Did it happen in a house, in a field, in a shed?'

She looks at me in amazement.

'You know about the shed?'

I nod. 'Yes Jane, the first time he attacked me, it was in a field, but I got away. The second time was different. There were two of them this time. They dragged me from my friend's garden in broad daylight, hauled me into a van and then drove to a shed in a field.'

I hold up my phone. 'The police will have both our statements on this recording—I know it's hard, but they need to know what happened, then they can help us.'

She looks at me with wide eyes.

'How did they get you into the shed, Jane?'

'I was walking home from work; I always come home for lunch; I don't work far away. A van drew up next to me and a man popped his head out of the window. He asked if I knew the way to Oxford; he was looking at a map, so I went over to show him.'

'Do you remember what he looked like?'

She shakes her head. 'He had sunglasses on and wore a hat.'

I nod. 'Then what happened?'

'The side of the van opened; a man pulled me inside and shut the door—it all happened so quickly.' Tears roll down her face—she stops, grabs a tissue and sobs into it.

'Don't cry, I'm going to help,' I murmur, hugging her to me. 'What did he look like?'

'He was wearing a black hood. On top was a black cap pulled down.'

'Anything else?'

'All I can remember is the smell of cigarettes.'

'And his face?'

'He wore a mask which made his voice sound horrible.'

'What happened then?'

She pauses and looks at me, tears stream down her face again. I hug her to me. 'Tell me, Jane, we need to know.'

'He put something over my eyes and did things to me; it was so awful. The van was going fast and when it stopped, he dragged me out of the van, pushed me into a shed, and pulled my pants down. I begged him to stop, but he only laughed and...'

'You're doing well, Jane, don't stop.'

'When he finished, the other man...'

She stops and bursts into tears.

'What happened then, Jane?'

'He hit me, then they took all my clothes off and they...' She shudders and looks at me. 'I begged them to stop, but they were so strong, I couldn't do anything...'

I bite my lip, pass her tissues from a box on the small table; she stops to wipe her face then carries on. 'Another man came. I think they called him Dick or Dicken, I'm not sure. Their voices sounded horrible, like Micky Mouse voices. He told them to put me in the van. Then I heard a tractor. Everything went quiet. I heard them moving around, then I heard a car, then a van driving away.'

'Was this in the statement you gave to the police?'

'Yes, it's in my head all the time, like a film that never stops.'

Jane's eyes are wide with fear; she's reliving it all over again. A shiver runs down my spine as she sobs.

'I pulled off the thing he covered my eyes with, put on my clothes and waited till the tractor had moved away, then I ran out, I ran and ran; I was so frightened. Then I went to the police.'

She sits with her arms wrapped tightly around her knees, slowly rocking backwards and forwards.

'This happened last year, didn't it?'

She nods and sits, hugging her knees to her chest.

'Why did you retract your statement? It would've helped the police; they might have caught them.'

'I was frightened; they said they'd do it again,' she mumbles. 'After it happened, I knew someone was following me.'

'Did this stop after retracting your statement?'

She nods.

It's getting late. I get up and look out of the window. Nicks moved the car it's outside the house, time for me to go.

'Don't worry. This nightmare will soon be over. If you think of anything, or just want to talk, call me; you have my number. Put it somewhere safe and don't tell anyone I've been here—okay? Not even your parents.'

She nods, puts the scrap of paper with my details in her pocket, and stands up.

'Try to stay inside for the next few days, unless you really have to go out. Tell your parents you're not feeling well, call work, tell them you're sick or something.'

She stares at me, a look of panic on her face. I sound just like Nick; he's always saying this to me, but I'm worried: I suppose he's also worried. I look at my notes; have I forgotten something? I've a feeling I have, but it's time to go.

I give her a hug. 'Please don't worry, it'll be over soon.'

She nods and walks with me to the door. 'Don't forget to call me?'

I nod and leave.

Once outside, I turn and look back at the house. Jane's peeping out from behind the living room curtain, looking at Nick in the car.

When I slide into the car, Nick's looking up at Jane. 'Is that her?' he asks.

I nod.

22

BETH & NICK

After Beth's visit to Jane...

'How did it go? What happened?' he mutters as we drive away.

The car is thick with smoke. 'What do you think?' I ask, winding down the window. 'She's a total wreck. You must get someone to watch the house until they catch these bastards.'

He frowns and drives faster. 'This is unofficial. How can I get her police protection if she doesn't report it?'

'You know why. She's terrified it will happen again. I listened carefully to her description of the two men who raped her.'

Drawing in a deep breath, I mutter, 'They could be the same men who attacked me.'

At first, he says nothing, just sits gripping the steering wheel, staring at the road ahead.

'So, what happened?' he suddenly asks.

'The driver of the van asked her how to get to Oxford. He had a map, so she offered to show him how to get there. That's when the other man opened a side door and pulled her inside the van. I've got it all down on this.' I hold up my phone. 'I asked her if it was alright to record it and she agreed.'

He says nothing, just grunts. 'What happened then?'

'They took her to a shed where they raped her, then they took off her clothes and raped her again. One of them was more violent than the other. It was only when the other guy arrived, they stopped, otherwise...'

The car goes around a sharp bend at a ridiculously high speed—I feel his thigh against me—he's going faster; he overtakes a car, there's another coming towards us.

'Nick, slow down, you'll kill us!'

We miss the car by the skin of our teeth. He slows down; I sit staring ahead, stunned at his stupidity.

'What's wrong with you, Nick?'

He doesn't reply.

I take a deep breath; I don't need this. It's bad enough talking about this stuff without having him to deal with.

I watch him out of the corner of my eye. 'That was really close—you could have killed us.'

He turns and looks at me. I'm struck by the expression in his eyes. He looks tired, as if he's had enough, or maybe he's just fed up with these unsolved cases.

'When did it happen?' he asks.

'A year ago, last September. The only reason she escaped was because a farm worker showed up in his tractor; if he hadn't, I hate to think what would have happened.'

We drive along in silence; he's deep in thought, I'm

thinking about my conversation with Jane. 'Nick, can they use the recording I made with my phone as evidence?'

He shrugs and says nothing.

'What about her clothes? Would the police ask her to keep the clothes she was wearing for evidence?'

'Shit. Bloody lights!'

He slams on the brakes. I'm flung forward.

'What's wrong with you?' I gasp. 'Stop driving like a maniac!'

He sits drumming his fingers impatiently on the wheel, cursing the lights. 'I thought you said she was naked. Did they test her body for traces of semen?'

'I just told you, Nick, the first time one of them raped her, she had her clothes on. He was in such a rush to—'

I can feel him watching me; then the lights change.

'Then what?' he asks, staring ahead at the road.

'They stripped her and raped her, then the other guy came, and they stopped. He told them...'

He brakes suddenly, just missing a car. 'I don't think she would keep the clothes. She probably went home, had a shower, then threw them away - that's what most victims do.'

'What, even if the police told her to keep them?'

He shrugs. 'They probably had all the evidence they needed.'

I sit listening to the recording — she doesn't mention the clothes or having a test, so I call her, but it goes to voicemail. I leave a message telling her to call me as soon as she can.

Nick parks in the street around the corner from our house. He stays in the car; I get out.

The officer watches as I walk into the garden and go inside; I'm sure he knows it's me. He must think I'm nuts.

As soon as I'm inside, I pull off the wig.

Then my phone rings.

'Yes?'

'It's me, Beth.'

'Jane, I'm so glad you called; I forgot to ask you something very important. Did you have tests taken at the station and what happened to the clothes you were wearing the day it happened?'

There's a long silence. 'Jane, are you still there?'

'I didn't want them,' she whispers.

'What, the tests?'

'Yes.'

'What about your clothes?'

She doesn't reply. 'Jane, what about the clothes you had on that day? Where are they?'

'I kept them.'

I can't believe it, she kept them!

'I waited for mum and dad to go to work at the bakery, then I buried them in the garden.'

I pace around the kitchen, pressing the phone tightly to my ear to block out the sound of someone knocking at the door. 'Can you get them by tomorrow? We need them for forensics.'

'Why?'

'Jane, if you have the clothes then we have evidence and we need all the evidence we can get, don't we?' I know I'm clutching at straws; I don't know how it works, but we must do something.'

She doesn't reply for a while, probably wondering when she can dig them up with no one seeing her.

'When my parents go to work, I can do it then,' she mutters. 'Do you want to come here, or shall I come to your place?'

The knocking on the door gets louder. I run and open it.

Nick rushes in. 'You took your time!' he growls. Then he motions to the phone. 'Who's that?'

I put my finger to my lip. He stops talking.

'Jane, can you hold on for a minute?' I mute the call and turn to Nick. 'She has the clothes. Shall we collect them from her place, or meet her somewhere?'

'I don't know why you're bothering, if they did the tests.'

'She said she didn't want the tests, but you can check with forensics, can't you?'

He shrugs. 'Do you still want to collect her clothes?'

'Yes.'

I sit watching him flick through his phone, then he stops.

'What about Irish? Tomorrow, in the pub near the train station in Oxford? I'll collect you at 11.30. That way she'll get home safely and so will you, and I won't miss my meeting.

'Yes, sounds good.'

'Sorry about that, Jane; I was just talking to DI Stephens. Can you meet me tomorrow in the pub next to the train station in Oxford, say around 11.00 in the morning?'

She says yes; I close my phone and turn to Nick.

'Can you take her clothes to forensics?'

He nods. 'But don't get your hopes up; it's been a long time; they might find nothing.'

Shrugging, I look at him. 'I'll send you a copy of the recording to use as evidence.'

He grunts and continues flicking through his phone.

For the first time in days, I feel we're really getting somewhere.

Then I think of Jane; she withdrew her statement.

Would forensics have checked the shed?

They must have—it was a crime scene. I turn to ask Nick, but he's on his way out of the door.

'Have to get back to work—talk to you later.'

He closes the door. I go into the kitchen, pour myself a large glass of wine, bung a pizza in the microwave and call Mum.

23

BETH & JANE

STATION PUB
Oxford

Nick should have been here ages ago—where is he? Surely, he hasn't forgotten us.

Jane's looking terrified; she just dug up vital evidence from her back garden and is now afraid someone was watching her.

'Don't worry, Jane,' I mutter, standing up to stretch my legs. 'Nick must've had an emergency; it happens all the time—I'll try one more time and if he doesn't answer, we'll get a cab. Okay?'

She nods and looks nervously around the pub. It's lunchtime and quite busy now. We're sitting in a corner away from the bar, but I can tell she's worried.

My call goes to voicemail. Maybe he switched his phone off, but why not text me? He could at least let me know if he's coming or not. I try one more time, then I call a cab.

Twenty minutes later, we're pulling up outside her house; she gets out and peers back at me.

'Call me, yes?'

'Of course, and please don't worry, Jane.'

She waves and runs to her house. I watch until she's safely inside, then get the cab driver to take me home. I'm hoping Nick will be there, but the house is empty.

I run upstairs to his bedroom; he's not there. His room faces the back, mine faces the front. From the window, I can see the young officer at the end of the garden. Now I know why Nick was chatting with him on the first day he came here; he knows him from the station.

Where the hell are you, Nick?

The officer in the front of the house smiles and watches as I get into Mum's car. I sit pretending to be on my phone while watching him through the car mirror. Just as I thought, he's on his phone. Let's hope he's calling Nick. I sit waiting for a call from Nick, but nothing happens. Then I have an idea. The police still haven't fitted CCTV along our street. I'll call them, find out what's happening, then ask if I can speak to Nick.

A bored-sounding woman answers the phone.

'Hi, this is Beth Papadakis, I was told you would fit CCTV in our street but I'm still waiting, can you tell me what's happening, this is very urgent, people's lives depend on it?'

'Sorry, I can't help. I'll leave a message for someone to get back to you.'

'But this is urgent; there must be someone there I can speak to.' I can feel myself getting angry and grit my teeth. 'I want to speak to someone now!'

The woman sounds frustrated and tells me to hold on.

A few minutes later, she comes back on the line. 'Sorry, I've asked around and nobody knows anything about it.'

'But this is ridiculous—someone must know.'

'I'll check with my colleagues and call you back. What's your number?'

I feel like screaming, but I give her my number, then ask if DI Stephens is there. She says she hasn't seen him. I turn on the ignition and start driving to Evesly. Then I remember the shed. I forgot to ask her if they'd checked for CCTV in the shed.

I call her back; she sounds annoyed and says she'll let someone know I called. Before she can hang up, I try one more time. 'Look, this is urgent; I need to know if CCTV is in that shed.'

I'm driving slowly waiting for her to find out; I don't want to get done for being on the phone while driving. Forensics were all over the place after what happened to me. Nick said this was normal procedure, but did anyone check for CCTV in the shed? All the terrible things that have happened there could be on camera. The shed is on Major Hudson's farm in one of his fields. He was in the army before he became an MP, so wouldn't he be hot on security?

The woman's voice cuts into my thoughts.

'Sorry, I can't access the case file, and even if I could, I'm not allowed to divulge this information over the phone; I suggest you come into the station and speak to someone.'

'But this is urgent!'

'As I said, I'll leave them a message about the CCTV in your street, and regarding your other question, you'll have to come into the station.'

I'm shaking with anger and slow right down. No call from Nick, no text—nobody knows where he is, not even the police. I try his number one more time—no reply.

Where the hell is he?

Major Hudson's farm is just a short distance from where I am, so I might as well see for myself if there is CCTV in the shed.

I drive for a few more minutes till I get to the field where the shed is; I turn off the engine and sit, listening. Apart from the sound of birds, there's no sound at all, just an eerie stillness about the place.

I climb out of the car and walk towards the shed. Suddenly I hear it, a rustling noise; I freeze.

Nothing happens. It must have been a breeze in the trees. Clenching my teeth, I duck under the police tape and open the door. With the light from my phone, I scan the walls and ceiling. Then I hear a tractor. This is what Jane must have heard. I shiver and quickly leave the shed.

It's a lovely warm sunny September day; what the hell am I doing here? I turn to walk back to my car when a flash of light from above in the trees catches my eye. It's probably just the reflection of the sun on something. I turn to leave, then it flashes again; it seems to come from the tree facing the shed.

Grabbing hold of a branch, I haul myself up. Mum's black dress catches on something. I tug it loose, there's a ripping sound, I groan and grip onto another branch.

The flash comes again; it's above me. Reaching up to push the branch away, I see something.

What the hell is that?

Hanging onto another branch, I hoist myself up—push away the leaves and freeze.

Fitted to the tree is a camera.

The tractor's coming closer— time to go.

Sliding into Mum's car, I quickly drive home.

24

BETH AT HOME

OXFORD

A TAP on the front door makes me jump.

Peeking through the hall window, I see the young police officer from the front garden looking at me.

Maybe it's about Nick.

I open the door quickly. 'Yes?'

'Sorry to bother you, I was told to let you know...'

'Nick!'

Oh my God, he's had an accident; that's why he didn't show up.

'Are you alright?' he asks, frowning.

'Has he... has he had an accident?'

He looks surprised. 'No, it's nothing like that. They came and fitted CCTV along the street. It was just after you left; they said to let you know and to say sorry it's late, but they've been very busy.'

'Does Nick know?'

'I haven't seen him, but he probably knows.' He gives me a smile, then turns and walks down the path.

Strange, but it makes me feel a little safer knowing CCTV is on our street; maybe what happened to the young officer galvanized them into action. Shame they didn't do it before, it would've saved us a lot of grief.

I feel like a drink but want to keep my wits about me. Then I spot Jane's bag of clothes still on the kitchen table where I left them. Mum's wardrobe is probably the safest place to hide them, which reminds me, I must call Mum.

Back in the kitchen, I sit flicking through my phone. I call Mum; it goes to voicemail. Where is everyone today? Still no news from Nick, and now Mum's not answering.

There's a tap on the door; I smile, expecting to see Nick when I open it, but it's not Nick; it's a delivery man with a large white box on wheels. I've ordered nothing, so it must be for Mum.

'Shall I bring it inside?'

The label on the box says it's for Mum.

I wonder what's inside? It must be heavy to be on wheels. Maybe a new lamp for the living room; she knows the other one broke during the fire.

'Yes, can you bring it into the kitchen?'

He nods, I turn to go into the kitchen, he pushes the trolley with the box inside.

The front door slams shut.

I turn—something's pressed over my mouth—I stumble; I feel dizzy. Then everything goes black.

25

BETH

Door's slam. I feel groggy—it's dark.

Where am I?

I'm rolling from side to side, I stretch out my hand to stop me, but it feels so heavy.

Then I remember the delivery man, the box for Mum. But it wasn't for her; it was a trap to get me, and it worked. My head hurts, I can't breathe, I must get out of here.

My hand travels to the sides of the box. There's nothing to pull. I wriggle my toes; I can feel my ankle boots, my skirt, my top—where's my phone?

There's a tearing sound above me, a shaft of light, then I'm being hauled out of the box. They quickly place a terrible smelly thing over my eyes. I try to resist, but it's no use. My arms are too heavy.

Focus, I must focus, I must get out of here, fast. I try to kick. Someone slaps me hard across the face—I stumble and fall.

'Move.'

The voice sounds distorted like a Micky Mouse voice.

I'm pushed, then dragged along; my hand touches something soft, it feels like carpet. Next minute I'm thrown onto something soft, I bounce.

Someone laughs. 'What shall I do with her, boss?'

Their voices sound weird.

'You know the procedure, strip her, tie her to the bed face down to begin with.'

I feel sick. I try to pull away, but it's useless. My legs have no strength; they must've drugged me.

Do something, I must do something—I must stop them.

I try to shout, but a sound like a croak comes out of me.

Someone laughs and pulls off my top.

My bra, he's undoing my bra. I push his hand away. He laughs, slaps me, then my bra is off.

I try one of my Krav Maga moves, but it's no use. I'm slapped again, harder this time.

I'm forced to lie face down. They tie my wrists with something.

It's so quiet.

My skirt's pulled off.

I can feel someone next to me.

Suddenly, I hear a door crash open.

'Stop, take your hands off her!'

'What are you doing here?'

'Just shut up and get off her.'

Nick? It's Nick. I'm shaking so hard I can hardly hear what they're saying. There's a lot of mumbling, then someone unties me and picks me up.

A door closes, then it's locked. I'm sat in a chair and that awful smelly thing's taken off my eyes. I cover my breasts with my hands and open my eyes. It's Nick, but he's looking at me strangely. His eyes are cold, his face is like a mask.

'I kept telling you to go,' he keeps mumbling.

What's wrong with him?

'Why didn't you listen to me?' he suddenly shouts. 'You could have gone to Athens, but no, you had to stay here. Now what can I do?'

'Get me out of here, of course.'

What on earth's wrong with him? The police must be here, but I can't hear them.

He's staring at me. He looks different. My legs feel weak, my mouth's dry.

'I need a drink, Nick.'

He doesn't move.

I look around the room. 'Where are the rest of the police?'

'Oh Beth, you think you're so clever, but you've got it all wrong.' He laughs, a nasty sarcastic laugh. His brown eyes are cold and devoid of any feeling. 'You still don't get it, do you? You always thought I was the nerd.'

'What are you talking about?'

What's wrong with him?

'Do something, Nick, for God's sake, get the police.'

He's staring at me. 'What am I going to do with you?'

He moves closer, his eyes move down my body. I'm naked except for my pants and boots.

'Nick, get me out of here.'

He grabs hold of me, pushes me onto a large sofa; he's on top of me, grabbing my breasts.

'What the hell are you doing? Get off me!'

His eyes are wild, like an animal.

In desperation, I raise my knee and kick him in the shin.

He falls off, then grabs me again. I kick him, this time in the face. Blood spurts all over me.

He stares at me. He looks crazy.

Someone shouts.

He freezes for a second, then gets off me, runs to the door, opens it and is gone.

There's the sound of a car; it must be him.

Stumbling over to the door, I turn the handle; it's locked. He locked it.

In desperation, I search for a door or a window, anything to escape from.

Then there's a loud bang, like an explosion, followed by screams and shouting.

I need something to cover myself—there's a long red runner on a nearby table; I tug it off and wrap it around me.

Behind one curtain is a small door; I peek out. Nobody's there. Gathering the red runner tightly around me, I make a dash for it.

Someone shouts. I try to run faster. I'm nearly out of the house when a side door opens. It's the police, guns at the ready.

Someone runs over and wraps a jacket around me. 'Come on, my car's outside; let's get you out of here.'

The young police officer takes me outside. Then, grabbing hold of me, she pulls me along with her.

'It's over there, not far to go.'

Opening the car door, she bundles me into the front, fastens my seat belt, then runs around and slides into the driving seat.

As her car pulls away, I can see police running all over the place.

I freeze. I know where we are.

She suddenly breaks to let a police van through.

The doors of the van open and a few seconds later, a man's hauled over to the van. He looks up and sees me watching him, his eyes narrow, then he's pushed inside.

26

Evesly Police Station

DCI THOMAS COMES into the room, sits down and peers at me over his glasses.

'I've had all the tests, so can I please go home?'

'It's best not to be alone at a time like this, Beth. Is there someone you can call, someone who can stay with you?'

I try to speak, but nothing comes out; all I can think of is Nick.

PC Jameson, the young officer sitting next to me, gives me a worried look. 'Are you okay?'

I look at her and nod. If she knew what I was thinking she'd be even more worried. 'I'm okay. I just want to go home.'

DCI Thomas looks at me for a few seconds, then turns to PC Jameson. 'Take Beth home and make sure you go inside with her. There's a constable outside the house and one at the back. She'll be safe for tonight.'

Turning to me, he says, 'I'll talk to you later, Beth.'

Fifteen minutes later, we're pulling up outside Mum's house.

'Are you sure there isn't someone I can call for you?' PC Jameson asks, following me inside the house.

'No,' I mutter, 'I'm fine.'

Then I realize I don't have my mobile. 'Where's my phone?' I mutter, walking into the kitchen, 'I'm sure I had it on me when...'

I stop and start thinking about the past few hours. An icy cold rush of rage washes over me—*I want to kill the bastards who did this*.

The PC gives me a startled look.

Was I talking aloud?

'I don't know,' she murmurs, raising an eyebrow and contemplating me thoughtfully. 'I'll check when I get back to the station; can I call someone for you?'

I suddenly feel exhausted. 'My Mum—can you let her know what's happened?'

She nods.

I scribble down her number on one of Jamie's new Pukka Pads lying on the kitchen worktop and hand it to her. 'She's in Spain; can you tell her what happened?' I point to the phone on the wall in the kitchen. She nods and walks over, picks up the phone and dials Mum's number.

I sit at the kitchen table watching her talk to Mum. I want to talk, but I can't, not now.

She talks quietly to Mum, telling her not to get upset, that I'm okay, then she quickly tells her what happened.

There's a long silence, then I hear Mum's voice. 'Tell her not to worry—I'll be there soon.'

PC Jameson puts down the phone. 'You heard that?'

I nod. 'Yes, thanks.'

She smiles. 'No problem, now let's make you a cup of tea and get you comfortable.' Picking up the kettle, she walks over to the sink to fill it. 'You've had a terrible time...'

'No, no thanks!'

She stops with the kettle mid-air. I can see she's worried, but I want her to go.

'I'm sorry,' I mumble, 'I just want to be alone.'

She sighs, puts the kettle down, takes a card from her pocket and hands it to me. 'Okay, but if you need anything, call me.'

I take the card and put it on the table in front of me.

She walks over to the door, then turns around. 'Don't worry, the police are outside; they're both armed, we're on high alert. I'll be back soon.'

I watch her from the living room window talking to the young police officer, then she gets in her car and drives away.

I feel so tired; I just want to sleep - I flop down on the sofa.

The next thing I know I'm wide awake and screaming—sweat's pouring down my face, my top's soaking wet.

Nick!

There's a tap at the door. 'Are you alright? It's PC Nuttall.'

I try to talk, but my voice sounds croaky. I run to the kitchen, splash my face with water.

He taps on the door again, this time louder.

Drying my face with a piece of kitchen paper, I shout, 'I'm coming.'

'I had a bad dream,' I mutter, opening the door. 'What time is it?'

'It's 3.40 in the morning; do you need any help?'

'No, I'm okay, thanks.'

I close the door, and after a few minutes, I hear him walk down the path. My chest feels tight—I can hardly breathe—all I see is Nick's face.

Slowly, I walk into the kitchen. My laptops on the kitchen table where I left it. I sit down; all I can think of is Nick.

A large knife on the draining board catches my eye. Slowly, I reach out for it.

———

I WAKE up with the knife in my hand—a door's opening.

'Beth, it's only me,' Mum calls from the hallway.

She's talking quietly to Jamie. I don't want him to see me like this.

Mum's walking into the kitchen. 'Don't worry,' she whispers, wrapping an arm around me. 'I told him you're not feeling well; he's gone to watch TV in my room.'

Relief floods through me as I hear him go upstairs. She takes the knife from my hand and places it in the drawer.

27

BETH & DCI THOMAS

OXFORD
Later that day...

I DON'T KNOW how long I've been laying here, but I can hear Mum and Jamie in the kitchen. Then it all comes back to me, Nick and the Major.

I must call Jane.

Mum has an extension next to her bed. Hauling myself off the sofa, I run as quietly as I can upstairs to her room. My call to Jane goes to voicemail; I leave her a message saying it's urgent, she must call me.

As soon as I put the phone down, the phone rings in the kitchen.

'Beth,' Mum calls from downstairs. 'It's DCI Thomas. Can you call him?'

'Yes,' I mumble.

His numbers on my phone, but I don't have my phone. Then I remember writing his number on one of the printouts I made; they should be in the drawer where I left them.

Just then, Mum calls up to say he's on the phone, and to pick up the phone in her room.

'Good morning, Beth, sorry to disturb you.' He hesitates for a minute, then carries on. 'I just remembered you don't have your phone; is it alright if I come round to see you, we need to have a chat, say in an hour?'

'Do we have to? Can't it wait?'

'No Beth, it can't wait. I need to talk to you now.'

I agree, what else can I do?

After having a shower, I peek out of the back-bedroom window and see Jamie and Mum in the garden having breakfast. I quickly get dressed and run downstairs.

'Mum!' Jamie shrieks, getting up and running over to me. He wraps his little arms around my waist. 'I've missed you Mum, are you alright?'

'Yes, I'm fine.' I give him a big kiss and hug him tight. 'I've missed you heaps.'

Mum smiles. 'We've made Spanish tortilla and salad—sit down and I'll cut you a slice.'

It's as if nothing happened. I sit listening to Jamie and Mum talking about what they've been up to in Spain. He's very tanned, they both are, they look incredibly healthy. I can tell Mum's worried, but she hides it well. Jamie thinks I've come down with a heavy dose of the flu, so finds nothing wrong with the way I look.

Mum goes into the kitchen to make coffee and leaves me chatting with Jamie about Spain.

Suddenly, there's a light tap at the front door.

'It's alright, it's DCI Thomas,' I call to Mum. 'I'll get it.'

I run to open the door. DCI Thomas peers over his glasses, clears his throat, and follows me inside.

'I'm sorry, but I need to take down a statement; it won't take long.'

'Yes, I know. Let's go into the living room.'

'You know, I've been on the force for twenty or more years,' he murmurs, following me into the living room. 'And I've seen nothing like this before.' He sits on one of the new chairs, pulls out his notepad, and looks at me.

'Have they got him?' I ask.

He peers at me over the top of his glasses. 'Sorry, what did you say?'

'Nick, where is he?'

He looks puzzled for a minute, then smiles. 'Don't worry about him, we saw him leave, he had a call from his brother-in-law in Italy, something urgent.'

I can't believe he just said that.

I sit staring at him.

Doesn't he know what he did?

He carries on talking as if nothing's wrong.

'His sister was in a head-on collision; she's in a terrible state. He's gone to see her, said it looks bad, they don't think she'll make it.'

He leans forward. 'Are you alright Beth? You don't look well. Shall I get you some water?'

I try to speak, but nothing comes out. I try again and mumble. 'Don't you know what happened?'

He looks startled and sits staring at me.

Tears stream down my face; I brush them away.

He grabs a tissue from a box on the sofa and hands it to me.

He doesn't know—he hasn't a clue what happened—he thinks it was just the Major and the other creeps.

I walk over to the window. The young police officer's outside as usual, but everything's changed. Nothing's the same anymore. I open my mouth, but the words won't come out.

'What is it Beth? Tell me?'

'Nick—he was there, at the Major's house—he's one of them.'

He looks at me in amazement. 'You've been through a terrible ordeal, Beth. Are you sure you're not confused?'

'I kicked him, I had too, he was going to...' I can't say it, for some reason I can't say it.

'What Beth?'

'He's just like the Major. If you don't believe me, check with forensics. I had his blood all over me.'

He stares at me in horror, then pulls out his phone and talks to forensics; he asks them to check the blood samples.

'It's not that I don't believe you, Beth, but I have to be sure.'

He gets up and stands looking out of the window, then after a few seconds he comes back, frowns and sits down again.

'You must tell me what happened, everything, alright?'

'I'm still trying to understand it myself. I trusted him with my life. How could he do this to me?'

'Take your time.'

Eventually, he has it all written in his notepad. I should feel better, but I don't. I still can't believe Nick would do this.

DCI Thomas gets up to go; I feel I've forgotten to ask him something, then I remember.

'Wait, how did the police know I was at the Major's house?'

He turns and looks surprised. 'I thought you knew.' He nods towards the garden gate where the young officer is standing. 'He had a funny feeling about the delivery man. After he left, he came and knocked on your door; he was suspicious when you didn't answer, so he climbed through your back-bedroom window, and that's when he knew something was wrong.'

'So, it's because of him they found me?'

'Well, yes, it was his quick thinking and you going on about the CCTV, if they hadn't installed it, they'd never have been able to trace the van.'

He stops talking, runs his hand through his grey speckled hair and shakes his head. 'What a terrible case this has turned out to be.'

I run outside to the startled young officer. 'Thank you so much for helping me.'

He looks surprised then looks over to the Inspector who's watching us from the front door. 'I just did my job,' he mutters.

I look at him closely. 'If you hadn't done what you did, who knows what would have happened to me?'

A slight smile has replaced the strained look on DCI Thomas's face. He walks over to us. 'Well, I'll be off.' Sliding his notebook back into his pocket, he turns and walks to his car. 'I'll see you tomorrow morning, at the station, around ten.'

I nod, go back inside and run upstairs to Nick's room.

His clothes are draped over the chair, his holdall bag's still on the floor; it all looks so normal. I rummage through the bag, not sure what I'm looking for, but I must look. *Maybe he's on drugs?*

But there's nothing but boxers, socks and shaving stuff. The room smells of him, his French cologne. It's as if he's still here, but he's not. He can't be, can he?

28

BETH & DCI THOMAS

EVESLY POLICE STATION
 10.00 am

Mum drops me off outside the police station; Jamie's in the front seat next to her. 'I'll call you when I finish!' I shout, waving to them. Jamie waves, Mum nods and drives off—I go inside.

DCI Thomas rushes out of his office; he probably saw us drive up from his window. His room overlooks the road.

He comes close, peers into my face as if judging if I'm up to what he has in store for me today.

'I have a lot to tell you, Beth.' Then his worried look returns. 'If you don't feel ready or you need professional help, I can arrange it.'

'No, I'm okay.'

'Well, you know it's there if you need it. Now about the other day—from your statement you say you recognized the man from the train. You said he was the man who attacked you in the field when you were on your way to Helen's house. Is that right?'

I nod.

'It all seems to have started with your train journey, Beth.'

'Yes, I was coming back from an interview in London.'

He scratches his head and looks at me. 'You never know what's going to happen, do you? It could happen to anyone; it was just unlucky your paths crossed.' He stops for a minute, then adds. 'You know he's got a record as long as your arm. The other one's just as bad, but Wiley, he's...'

As soon as he mentions their names, I feel the blood drain from my face.

He stops talking, as if changing his mind. 'You don't have to worry about them anymore. They're in police custody.'

'What about the Major, and the other man?'

'We've done a thorough check on the Major.' He grimaces slightly, as if there's a nasty taste in his mouth. 'It all started in Cyprus; he was in the army, did you know?'

'Yes, Nick told me.'

How strange it sounds to hear his name coming from my lips. It sounds so normal, but it's not. Nothing's normal anymore, everything's changed.

'Beth, are you listening?'

I nod.

He grunts, looks at me closely, then carries on talking.

'There were rumors, terrible rumors about the Major. Of course, it was all covered up by the old boy network, you know—he's such a respectable man—how could anyone think that of him, he's an MP. Anyway, there were reports of rapes and assaults in the area he lived in Cyprus and many retracted statements of rape like here.'

He stops and peers at me over his glasses.

My chest feels tight, I try not to think, but it's all coming back, the field, the shed, the Major, Nick.

'Are you okay, Beth? Shall I stop?'

I feel myself shaking; I clench my hands into fists. 'Carry on, I need to know.'

'Well, Wiley and Jonas are both squealing to save themselves, but I don't think it'll help them much; they'll be going down for a long time. The girls were mainly local girls.' He shakes his head and frowns. 'The Major's long-time buddy Dicken, another nasty piece of work, used to flatter them and butter them up, that was his specialty, give them a few drinks and get them tipsy, that's how he got them into his car. They were hanging around pubs looking for excitement—he was good looking, just what they needed, or so they thought—he added drugs to their drinks to sedate them.' He shakes his head and looks at me. 'And as we know, the rest was easy.'

He stops and peers at me, then starts again. 'His good looks took them in—a right charmer, that one. Most didn't have a clue what had happened. Then Wiley and Jonas would drop them off at various locations.'

'How did they get away with it?'

He runs his fingers through his grey speckled black hair. 'They had someone inside, Beth, someone to take care of things.'

I look at him in horror. Now it all falls into place.

'You mean Nick?'

He nods. 'And we're also running checks on the Detective Superintendent; seems he was a good friend of the Major. He's just taken early retirement and back living the good life in Northern Cyprus.'

'So why did he do it? How can anyone change so much? Maybe he's on drugs?'

'You mean Nick?'

I nod.

'I don't know if he's on drugs, but the money must have had something to do with it. You know the Major has many influential friends who share his taste in, shall we say, *entertainment*—they pay a lot for this, so the Major gladly obliges. With Nick onside, the rest was easy.'

'I still can't believe Nick would do this,' I mumble, as if to myself. 'Nobody can change so much, can they?'

He gazes out of the window, probably thinking of Nick. They were close; he's known him since he was a boy. It must have come as a terrible shock to him.

Taking off his glasses, he cleans the lenses with a cloth, then puts them back and looks at me. 'Wiley and Jonas are trying to get off by spilling the beans. In Jonas's statement he says the girls they found for the Major were usually very young and ready to party. Most never knew what had happened; if they did, they coerced them into saying nothing about it. As with Jane's case. Those brave enough to make one found out the hard way and soon retracted their statements.' He stops and looks at me. 'And that's why the Major came down so hard on you as you were about to ruin everything for him.'

I sit thinking of Nick. 'You know, I asked him to take me to see Jane. I was so desperate to find something, anything, that would help catch these people. He said he could get into trouble, but he took me to see her.'

I stop, he says nothing, so carry on. 'You probably know, I gave him a copy of the recording of the conversation I had with Jane. It should come in useful as evidence. I still have the clothes she was wearing when it happened.'

I look at him; he nods, as if he's taking it all in. 'You already know I met Jane in the pub next to the train station in Oxford. Nick was supposed to meet us there, but he didn't show up. I asked him to take Jane's clothes to be tested...'

DCI Thomas gets up and walks over to the window. 'He fooled us all, Beth. We never received your taped conversation with Jane.'

He turns around, a worried look on his face. 'Beth, I need to tell you something.'

He walks back to his desk, sits down, fumbles with some papers, then looks at me. 'Jane left a note for her parents saying she was going around the corner to the shops. She said she'd be back soon, but she never came back. It was the same day, the day it happened to you. They think she was meeting someone.'

'But she would never go with anyone unless she trusted them.'

Then I know what's happened.

'Nick - he's the only person, other than me, that she'd trust. She saw him when I was leaving her house; she knew what he looked like, if he called at her house or phoned her...'

DCI Thomas suddenly stands up and starts pacing around the room.

'Sorry to be the one to tell you, Beth, but there's still a chance we'll find her, if you can think of anything, anything that might help.' He stops and frowns. 'And do nothing alone, okay?'

I nod.

Once outside, I see Mum in her little yellow Fiat waiting for me. She gives me a worried look; Jamie just thinks I've visited the police about the fire, so doesn't find it strange that I should keep seeing DCI Thomas.

After a quick cup of coffee at home, I ask Mum if I can borrow the car.

She gives me one of her looks. 'Beth, don't you think you've done enough?'

'I want to get Jamie a present, maybe a new pair of trainers, as a surprise.'

She frowns. 'He doesn't need new trainers; I bought him some in Spain.'

'Mum, I need to get something for him.'

She sighs. 'Okay, but don't be long—be back for lunch.'

I glance at the clock on the kitchen wall; it's nearly twelve that gives me an hour.

29

MAJOR OLIVER'S FARM

Mid-day

BLUE and white police tape surround the Major's farm; I don't want to be seen so park a little further back along the road. Then I see DCI Thomas, he's spotted me.

He ambles over to the car and eyes me suspiciously.

'I thought you were going home?'

'I did. I went home, had a coffee, then I thought a drive would do me good.'

He exhales loudly. I know he doesn't believe me. He peers into the car. 'So, why come back here?'

I get out of the car and stand looking around.

'Speak up. Tell me why you're here.'

He isn't a fool. He has a good idea why I'm here, so I tell him.

'It's just a feeling I have. I could be wrong.'

He taps his foot impatiently, lights a cigarette, inhales deeply, then looks at me.

'Okay, Nick saved me from the Major but then...'

I can't bring myself to say it, so I stop, take a deep breath and start again.

'I've been thinking, maybe Nick was already at the Major's house. Do you remember when I told you Nick was supposed to collect us from the pub in Oxford, but he never arrived?'

He nods impatiently.

'Nick dropped me off at the pub around 11.00 am in his car. I didn't have a car, so when he didn't come, I took Jane home in a cab.'

'And?'

'Well, after dropping Jane off at home, I kept trying to call Nick to find out why he hadn't collected us, but each time I called, it went to voicemail. This went on for hours...'

All the time I've been talking, he's been watching me closely.

'So, you think she could be here?' he asks, looking over at the house, a questioning look on his face.

I shrug my shoulders.

'Well, say something,' he snaps.

'Have you searched all the rooms?'

He frowns and starts rubbing his chin. 'Yes, we searched the house. We found video footage and other items, but nothing else.'

I have a feeling of dread as I look over at the old Cotswold farmhouse.

'If he brought Jane here.' He stands surveying the house. 'Where do you think he would take her?'

'I'm not sure, but there are lots of rooms. It's such a large house she could be anywhere—in the cellar, in the attic.' My voice trails off as I remember things I want to forget.

He strides over to the house. 'Search all the rooms, cupboards, the attic, garage, cellar. We're looking for a young woman with red hair. Be as quick as you can and shout if you find anything.'

He comes back, lights another cigarette and eyes me thoughtfully.

It's times like this I feel the need for a cigarette. I watch him take another deep drag.

I usually carry a pack or have one in the car for emergencies. Opening the car door, I search in the glove compartment.

Where are the damn things?

He thrusts a packet of Marlboro through the window. 'Here, have one of these.'

I take one and murmur thanks. He nods and strolls back to the house.

For a few minutes I watch him, then I light up and take a few drags. I have an eerie sense of dread. I know that feeling of desperation, hoping someone will come and save you. I think of Jane and shiver—she must be so frightened.

The minutes tick by, then I think of Mum at home worrying about me. If I don't text, or go home soon…

DCI Thomas suddenly appears at the front door; behind him a man's carrying something wrapped in a blanket.

I run over, a bit of red hair's poking out of the blanket.

'Don't worry,' he mutters. 'She's okay. I'm taking her to the hospital. You go home your mum will be worried sick.'

Jane's out cold.

I run back to my car, call Mum saying I'm okay and will be home soon, then follow them to the hospital in Oxford.

After what seems ages, DCI Thomas comes out of the emergency room and walks over to where I'm sitting.

'Is she hurt?' I blurt out as soon as he sits down.

He's watching me closely. 'I'll be in touch. Now you go home and get some rest.'

'Was she given chloroform?'

He nods. 'Now go home.'

I'm just about to get into my car when I see him running towards me.

'Beth,' he shouts, stopping just to draw breath. 'Did Nick ever talk to you about Cyprus?'

I stand looking at him, wondering what's happened. 'Not really, he just said the Major was in the army there. Why do you ask?'

He scratches his head. 'I'm not sure.' He ruffles his hair and sighs. He looks tired. 'We've confiscated all the video footage, so we'll soon be able to identify the people involved.' A slight smile appears on his face. 'A lot of wealthy and influential heads are going to roll soon, Beth.' He gives me a nod, walks over to his car, then turns around. 'Oh, they found your phone; it's at the police station.'

'Thanks! I'll pick it up tomorrow.'

I suppose I should feel better, but I don't.

Back to school

Next morning, we walk along in silence. Jamie drags his feet, something he never does. I talk about what we'll do at the weekend, he just ignores me.

'I'm meeting Helen tomorrow; she's popping over for a few days.'

He doesn't answer.

'Shall I bring you something back from London?'

He shrugs. I don't want to get his hopes up, but I'm viewing a couple of apartments and I also have an interview lined up in London.

We're at the school gates. He keeps looking at the ground. I feel dreadful. He trudges into the school. No wave, no smile. I walk home feeling terrible. Even his first day at nursery school in Athens was better than this.

30

BETH & HELEN

LONDON
Kensington Gardens

THE PARK'S a blanket of leaves all waiting for me to run and walk in them. It's the sound of crunching they make I love; it's something I've always done and always will, no matter how old I get.

Spiky green conkers, autumnal sunshine, who could ask for anything more. A large green conker pokes out from under the leaves; I grab it and prize it open. Inside is a shiny brown conker resting on a bed of white velvet. I roll it around in my hand, then tuck it in my pocket for Jamie; he loves conkers.

Sighing contentedly, I inhale the scent of the park; it brings back many happy memories of my childhood. Happy days. The long days of summer are ending, autumns in the air.

'You look as if you're doing an ad for Autumn watch in

London,' Helen laughs, running over. 'It's just like old times, isn't it? I think you were happy when you lived here, weren't you?'

'Yes, but that was a long time ago; I was much younger. I used to love the old swings. This new playground is far grander, but I still prefer the old one.'

'Yes, because it holds happy memories for you.'

She loops arms with me, and we walk to the open-air café beside the children's playground. 'It's part of growing up. We always yearn for the years when we were young, but we should really focus on the present.'

'Very profound Helen; anymore where that came from?'

She laughs. 'Yes, now grab a seat and I'll get the drinks—hot chocolate or coffee?'

'Coffee.'

It's not too busy, just a couple of tourists sitting eating a take-away meal and a mum with a pram reading a book.

'So, what do you think of the apartments we saw?' Helen asks, placing a tray of hot drinks and chocolate muffins on the wooden table.

'I'm not sure. They're all so expensive.'

Breaking off a piece of muffin full of chocolate buttons, I sit looking at it, then pop it in my mouth. 'I've an interview this week for a job in a newspaper. I only hope it's better than the last one I went to.'

She frowns. 'Don't worry about money; I can help.'

'Thanks for the offer, but we'll be okay. I just need a job.'

'You still have your apartment in Athens. Why not sell it?' She stops drinking and looks at me. 'Are you still refusing to take money from Alex?'

'He still lives there, and I don't want to sell it, it's my stake in Athens. You never know, we might need it one day.'

'Well, the money's always there if you need it.' She sits sipping her hot chocolate while flicking through her phone. 'You know if positions were reversed, and it was me, I'd take it. If it hadn't been for James helping me out with some of his inheritance, I'd probably have nothing, so if you need it, take it, Beth—it's only money.'

I laugh and hug her. 'You never know, I might take you up on that. Now enough about me. How's Theo?'

At first, she says nothing, just sits sipping her drink. Then her face changes. She looks serious. 'Things haven't been good for some time; he's changed so much.'

'You should have said something. I didn't know.'

'It'll probably pass. At least I have my job and James to talk to. I don't know what I'd do if he wasn't there.'

She smiles, then changes the subject. 'So, which apartment did you like best? The one with the garden, with the little water feature? It was nice, but dark inside, don't you think?'

'Yes, the garden flat was lovely, but I don't really like basements. The one in the mansion block is more my thing. It's close to where we used to live, it's full of light, and the rent's not too high. All I need now is to get that job!'

'Don't worry, you'll get one soon. What about your mum? Is she staying in Oxford?'

'I don't think so, what with the recent events; I think she wants to go away. She loves Oxford, but not during the long winter months. I think she's looking for a place in Spain or Greece.'

'Wow! She really has had enough. What about Nick? Have you heard anything?'

I catch my breath. The sound of his name makes me shiver. 'No, come on, let's go back to your hotel; you've a plane to catch, remember?'

She tugs at my arm. 'Beth, do they know where Nick is? Have they told you?'

I shake my head.

We walk to the park exit, opposite the Hilton Hotel and Queensway tube station. My hands are deep in my pockets, holding the conkers I collected for Jamie.

'Come on, Beth, you must have heard something.'

I shrug.

'What about that Inspector guy you're always talking about?'

'You don't give up do you?'

'No, because I know you Beth.'

'Okay, I had a call from DCI Thomas this morning. He asked me to pop into the station today, but as I was coming to meet you, I said I'd see him later.'

'Did he tell you what it's about?'

'No, he wouldn't say anything. He said he'd tell me later, when I go to Evesly.'

'Why didn't you tell me this morning?'

'Why? It's probably nothing. You know how they love to exaggerate things. There's probably been a sighting of him somewhere. Maybe he's in Europe, who cares? I really don't want to know.'

Why did I say that?

Of course, I want to know where he is. I often think I see him; I get a whiff of his cologne, but when I look, he's not there.

She has that worried look on her face again. 'But what if he's still in Oxford?'

'So, what if he is? I don't think he'll be bothering me again, do you?'

She gives me a funny look, pulls me across the road before the traffic lights change, then we walk to her hotel.

It's only a few minutes' walk from the park so we don't have far to go.

As soon as we enter her room, she rushes to the loo. I go onto the balcony to take in the amazing view. If I had an apartment at the top of a block with views like this, I'd never leave London.

A few minutes later, Helen joins me. We stand admiring the view; then she turns to me, an anxious look on her face. 'Beth, it could be dangerous if you stay here. Why don't you come back to Athens? Jamie can go back to his old school. Maybe you can get your old job back. You never know, it's worth trying.'

She knows I'm worried about Jamie and his new school; of course, he'd be happier back in Athens, but we can't go back, not now.

'Beth, did you hear me?'

'Sorry, I was miles away.'

'Does Alex know what happened? He often calls me and says he's worried about you and Jamie. I don't know what to say. I always try to change the subject.'

I nod. 'Yes, I've also had a few calls from him, but I haven't answered. Why should I, after what happened in Athens?'

'Come on, let's not get depressed. I'll be leaving for the airport soon. Let's go to the bar and have a drink.'

'Yes, only two days in London. Business must be good.'

She laughs and snaps her expensive looking bag shut.

'It will be very good if I get this contract. That's why I'm here, and to see you, of course.'

'Good for you, you deserve it.'

'Thank you, Beth, it's really very easy; I promote their hotel by offering discounts, then I get commission from them.'

As we walk to the elevator, she pauses. 'Don't forget to take the coach home, not the train, okay, promise?'

I nod, but I have no intention of taking the coach back to Oxford.

31

BETH

LONDON
 Early evening

We have time for a quick drink then I walk with Helen to Bayswater tube station. She takes the train to Heathrow Airport; I walk to Paddington Station.

It's only a ten-minute walk and soon I'm passing the guy handing out the free edition of the Evening Standard and a guy dishing out discount vouchers for the local McDonalds.

I walk down the little side street into the station, which is packed with people, it's the rush hour in London, so not the best time to travel.

Now to check if my train's running on time. I search the overhead board - there it is platform 3 leaving at 6.05 pm, only five minutes to go.

I make my way to the platform, all the carriages are full, quite the opposite from the last time I was here. Suddenly I picture that fateful day, that horrible man sitting beside me. I shudder and force myself to stop thinking of him.

There's a spare seat by the window so I quickly sit down. A few minutes later there's the familiar clank and groan of the train as it leaves the station.

If I hadn't been in such a rush to catch the train that day, if I'd waited and caught the next train - then I stop - it did happen, so deal with it.

I force myself to stop thinking and press my face up against the window and peer at the passing warehouses and backs of old Victorian houses which at some time must have been beautiful but now just look drab. Sometimes you can catch a glimpse of the lives of those who live there, but they can also see us, something we tend to forget. I wonder what secrets the people in these old houses hold.

The train's packed with people heading home from the city after a hard day's work. Heads are buried in iPhones and iPads, a few read the free London newspaper, others just sit with their eyes closed.

The journey passes quickly, an hour after leaving Paddington the train pulls into Oxford, I hurry home.

'Mum, Jamie, I'm back.'

No reply, where is everyone?

I walk from room to room, but nobody's here.

A few minutes later the front door opens and in comes Mum.

'Hey Mum, where's Jamie?'

She gives me a puzzled look. 'Isn't he with you?'

'Why should he be?' Then I look at her face and my heart skips a beat. 'Did you collect him from school?'

She runs over and grabs me. 'He said he was going with you to London.'

'But...'

My legs feel weak, I feel dizzy. 'When did he say that?'

'This morning, he was in the kitchen having breakfast, I

had an early appointment with the estate agent. He said he was going with you.'

I look at her in horror, her face crumples, her lips start trembling. 'He didn't come with me, I thought you'd taken him to school.'

Her face is ashen, tears stream down her cheeks.

I stand staring at her, frozen with fear. 'So, if he didn't go to school, where is he?'

'Have you tried his mobile?'

Before I can reach my phone, Mum's already calling him, no reply, it goes to voicemail.

'Call the police, tell them he's missing,' she shrieks.

DCI Thomas isn't at the station, so I speak to someone who says he'll be round to see us soon.

Mum's sitting at the kitchen table, frowning. 'This isn't like Jamie. He must be in such a state - why don't you call Helen?'

'Helen! What can she do? She's on a plane on her way back to Athens.'

She grabs her car keys and rushes to the door.

'Where are you going?' I demand, running after her.

'I'm going to look for him, see if I can find him.'

I pull her back. 'Don't, the police will be here soon, wait and see what they say.'

'But we must do something, we can't just sit here, can you think of anywhere he'd go?'

Then a terrible thought comes to me. I grab my phone and text Helen.

Jamie's missing call me as soon as you land.

Ten minutes later PC Arnold arrives, I take him into the kitchen, he glances at Mum who points to a chair.

'Now tell me exactly what happened?' he says, taking out his notebook.

Mum and I look at each other.

'Has the little lad been under a lot of pressure recently?'

I tell him about the firebomb, how he hates his new school and wants to go back to Athens and that DCI Thomas is dealing with the case and to check with him if he needs anything.

'What are you going to do?' Mum asks, impatiently.

He looks at her then at me. 'I'll need a recent photo of the boy.'

Mum pulls out her phone and shows him one taken in Spain.

PC Arnold nods and hands her a card. 'You can send it to me here.'

He walks to the door then turns. 'Keep your phones with you at all times.'

Mum follows him out. 'Get them to search the streets of Oxford.' Then in a lower voice she adds. 'He may be sitting somewhere, frightened to come home, he's only eleven, he'll be twelve next week.'

PC Arnold nods and leaves.

32

OXFORD

Where is Jamie?

I HAVE visions of Jamie wandering around Oxford, not wanting to come home, worried I'll be angry. Then I think of what could happen to him. What time is it? When will Helen land? Oh, this is crazy, what can she do, he's in Oxford not Athens. But maybe he did call her. Maybe he left her a message.

Mum's making tea, she says nothing, but her face says it all.

A couple of hours later my phone rings, it's Helen.

'Beth, have you heard from Jamie?'

'No, I was hoping you might know something.'

'But why would I know? Why would he call me?' She pauses for a minute. 'Have you tried his dad? He might have called him.'

'He's the last person I want to talk to.'

I start pacing around the kitchen rubbing my forehead, trying to think. 'And why would he call Alex? He never had time for Jamie when we were in Athens, he was always too busy running around being the hotshot lawyer.'

'Beth, when we were in the park you said Jamie hates the school and wants to go back to Athens.'

'Yes.'

'Shall I give Alex a call? He might know something. What do you think?'

'I don't know why he should know, but if you think it would help.'

A few minutes later, my phone rings. It's Helen.

'Beth, I've something to tell you. Now don't worry and don't get upset.'

'What is it?'

'Jamie's here. He's with his dad.'

'What?'

I can't believe it, he can't be in Athens. How could he get there?

As if reading my mind, she quickly adds. 'He called Alex, told him about the fire, about going to Spain with your Mum. Beth, he told him he hates the school and that he wants to come back to Athens with you.'

I sit, listening in horror. It's my worst nightmare come true.

'Alex is furious you didn't tell him, and that's why he did this.' She pauses for a moment. 'Didn't you miss him this morning? I thought you walked him to school?'

'I do, but as he wasn't downstairs, I thought Mum had taken him. She said she was getting up early to see the agent, so I just presumed she had taken him. She said he was up early and told her he was going to London with me, and she believed him. He must have left for the airport soon after because when I came down, he wasn't there.'

I try to breathe slowly — I still can't believe he would do

this. I stare out of the kitchen window, not seeing anything, just thinking of Jamie. He could have left me a note, he could have sent me a text.

Then I think of Alex.

'Why did Alex send him a ticket? Why didn't he call me or at least text me? He knew I'd be going out of my mind with worry when I discovered he wasn't here.'

Then a thought comes to me. 'How did they allow him on the plane by himself? I had to accompany him through security at the airport to make sure a flight attendant took him on board. I had to complete loads of forms. They're very particular about this. How did he do it?'

'Jamie was lucky. It seems a friend of Alex's, another lawyer, was returning to Athens. Alex asked him to accompany Jamie on the flight. He spoke to the authorities, sent them all the relevant documentation, giving his consent. He is his father and he's a very good lawyer. Jamie was desperate for help, so he asked his dad and he arranged it all.'

'So, when I took him to school yesterday, he'd already planned it with Alex?'

She grunts. 'Beth, try to relax, get some sleep. I'll see him in the morning. We'll have a chat, then I'll call you.'

I say nothing. I know she's trying to help, but I feel so angry. I wish I'd hidden his passport, but how was I to know he'd do something like this? He's only eleven, well, nearly twelve.

'I'm just so angry. At least Alex could have texted me. I want to speak to Jamie — put him on the phone, Helen.'

'Leave it Beth, Alex said he's in his room, he must be exhausted. It's just gone 11.00 in the evening here, so he's had a long day.' She pauses, then adds. 'Alex has a big court case tomorrow, he...'

'I'm getting the next plane to Athens; we'll sort everything out when I get there.'

'No Beth, it's too late. Stay there, go to bed. I'll call you in the morning.'

I quickly tell Mum that Jamie's okay, that he's at his dad's. She shakes her head in disbelief.

'But how did he get there?'

'He asked his dad, and he arranged it,' I shout, running upstairs for my passport.

I'm on my laptop searching for a flight but there aren't any. September is the high season for travel to Greece. There are no flights, so how on earth did his dad get him one? Helen can do it. She's in the trade, but she told me to wait until tomorrow.

I inhale deeply and go downstairs. Mum and I make tea and toast, talk about schools, then go to bed. But sleep evades me. I lay thinking about Jamie. I must find him another school, or move somewhere else, somewhere he likes, but not Athens.

Then I think of DCI Thomas. Why did he want to see me? It must be something about Nick. Maybe they know where he is?

I fall into a restless sleep dreaming of Nick, then wake up screaming his name.

I sit up gasping for breath and see Mum staring at me.

'Are you alright, Beth?'

I sit up and look around.

Nick was here, he was in this room — he was looking at me.

33

OXFORD
8.00 am in the morning

I WONDER if Helen's up. They're two hours ahead in Athens, so she should call me soon.

After coffee and toast, I drive to the police station. I'm informed by the officer at the desk that DCI Thomas has just arrived and to wait in reception.

Fifteen minutes later, he tells me to go in.

I knock and peer round the door. 'Sorry about yesterday, I was in London, then when I arrived home Jamie...'

He waves his hand for me to come in. 'I was out anyway. Something came up, close the door and sit down.'

I tale a sit seat opposite him. 'Did you talk to PC Arnold yet?'

He's watching me over his glasses, which have slid down over his nose. He pushes them up. 'Yes, I heard all about it from him this morning. Well, at least the boy's safe.' As an afterthought, he asks. 'Would you like a coffee?'

'No thanks, I just had one at home.'

He shuffles some papers on his desk, then stands up and starts pacing around the room.

'I've something to tell you, Beth.' He stops and looks at me. 'There's been a sighting of Nick.'

My heart suddenly leaps into my mouth. I knew this would happen. I sit staring at him, waiting for him to say something.

He walks back to his desk, picks up a piece of paper, and sits down to read it.

Why is he taking so long? He knows where he is, why draw it out?

'So, where is he?' I growl impatiently.

He instantly looks up. 'It's only a sighting. We have to check it out.'

I sit clenching my hands together staring at him.

'I'm waiting for more information.'

Then he frowns, as if deciding to tell me or not. 'He was seen at a petrol station in the Lake District. Someone recognised him from a photo in one of the old daily newspapers.'

So, he is still here. I remember him saying something about his parents—he said they'd moved up north. Maybe he's staying with them?

He looks at me thoughtfully. 'Don't worry. I just thought you should know.'

Well, of course I should bloody well know.

I get up and start pacing around the room.

He's staring at me. Did I just think that or say it?

I try to stay calm, but inwardly I'm screaming. After what that bastard did to me, of course, I should know where he is.

I shrug and sit down. 'I didn't think he'd still be here.'

'He doesn't have much choice, does he, Beth?' He looks at me closely, then carries on. 'We have the train and bus stations covered and the airports and ports. I don't think he'll be going anywhere.'

He grunts and begins typing on his laptop, then gets something out of his drawer. It's a tracking device.

He walks over to me. 'This is just to be on the safe side, Beth. Can you roll up your sleeve?'

This is just what Nick did, but with my phone. It doesn't seem so long ago. I often wonder why he did that. Why should he care if they caught me again?

I roll up my sleeve. 'But you just said he's in the Lake District, so why do I need this?'

'It's just a precaution.' He peers at me over his glasses. 'You can still go to Athens with this on you.'

'I'm trying to find a job and a place to live, somewhere Jamie likes. If he's happy, that's all that matters, but definitely not Athens.'

He frowns and gives me a serious look. 'It might be a good idea to spend a bit of time in Greece, till this is over.'

'And what if Nick follows me there?'

He sits with a thoughtful look on his face. 'Don't worry, we'll get him. It's just a matter of time.'

We sit in silence for a few minutes, each with our own thoughts, then I get up to leave.

He looks up at me, a look of concern on his face.

'Think about what I said, okay?'

I nod and leave him rummaging through his desk.

Outside the police station, I check my phone. No call or message from Helen. It's 10.20 in the morning, so 12.20 in Athens. What the hell is she doing? I try her number. It goes to voicemail.

I'll give Tula a call. Maybe she knows.

She picks up after the second ring. 'Hi Tula, I need to

speak to Helen. She said she'd call me this morning, but she hasn't.'

'But Beth, she's on her way to London.'

'What?'

I can't believe it. Why didn't she call me?

'Which flight is she on?'

'She should land at Luton at 1.45 our time, so 11.45 your time.'

'Thanks Tula.'

I hail a passing cab and ask him to put his foot down. This is an emergency.

On the way home, I text Helen saying I'll be at the airport to meet them, then I call Mum.

'Good news, Mum, get the car ready. We're going to the airport to meet Jamie and Helen.'

34

Luton Airport

I STAND SEARCHING everyone coming through customs. At last, I see Helen's long brown hair and Jamie's dark curly head bobbing alongside her — I run over to meet them.

Jamie throws his arms around me. 'Sorry Mum, I didn't mean to worry you, but I hate that school.'

I'm so happy to see him that my anger disappears at once. 'I've been so worried,' I murmur, holding him tight.

Mum comes over and looks at him. 'We've been sick with worry about you, Jamie.' Then she ruffles his hair and gives him a kiss. 'Never do that again, promise?'

He nods.

Helen's hovering behind him, a satisfied look on her face.

'Thanks Helen, I...'

'Don't be silly. You'd have done the same for me. Anyway, I forgot to do something in London, so I had to come back, won't be a minute, I just have to make a call.'

I leave her to make her call.

Fifteen minutes later, we're in the car driving home. Mums in the back with Jamie, Helen's in the front with me. Jamie's so tired he's fallen asleep on Mum's shoulder.

I nudge Helen. 'He's asleep, so tell me, what happened?'

Her voice is so low that I can hardly hear what she's saying.

'I told him he wouldn't have to go back to the school in Oxford, and that you weren't angry.'

'But where is he going to go?'

'Beth, it's the only way I could get him on the plane.'

Jamie stirs; we stop talking and resume when he's gone back to sleep.

'Did you see Alex?' I ask as quietly as I can.

'Yes, he was on his way to court. I think he was relieved to see me.'

I grip the steering wheel tight. 'I'll bet he was still the same old Alex. Who is he defending this time?'

Helen shrugs and yawns, her eyes droop. We drive along in silence, then she nods off.

As soon as we arrive back at Mum's, Jamie falls asleep watching TV. Helen goes for a lay down, and Mum and I cook cannelloni for dinner.

Suddenly, my phone rings. It's a woman from the estate agents in Queensway, the one who showed us the apartments.

'Hello, I'm calling to let you know we have the keys for your apartment. When will you be collecting them?'

'What?'

'You just called us.' She sounds surprised. 'You paid six months' rent in advance for that apartment in the mansion block.'

'There must be some mistake.' I look at Mum and frown. 'You must have the wrong number.'

'No, this is the number...'

'Sorry, you've made a mistake.'

I close my phone.

Mum looks at me questioningly. 'Who was that?'

'The estate agent in Queensway, they said they have the keys to my apartment. They wanted to know when I was collecting them.'

'But didn't you go there the other day, with Helen?'

'Yes, we looked at a couple of apartments, but I didn't rent one. How could I? I'm not working. Someone else must have looked at it. She made a mistake and called the wrong number.'

As soon as Helen wakes up from her nap, I tell her about the agent calling from Queensway.

'She got the wrong number. Someone else must have seen it after us.'

'Is it that apartment you liked, the one in the mansion block?'

I nod.

She laughs. 'Then take it.'

'Are you crazy?' Didn't she hear me right? 'I didn't send them any money; she made a mistake?'

She suddenly laughs. 'But it is yours, Beth.'

Then the penny drops.

Before I can say anything, she comes over and sits next to me. 'At least this way you'll know if you like it, won't you?'

'But Helen...'

She holds up her hand. 'I got a very good deal. I said it needs a lot of work, the rooms are too small - blah blah blah. They've had it on their books for some time, so if you don't mind decorating it...'

'Of course, I don't.'

'Great, and if you change your mind, you can always stay with me, or sell the apartment in Athens. Why should Alex have it all to himself? You can buy another apartment.'

She's right. We can always sell the apartment and with my half of the money I can buy something else. Alex is rolling in money, so it won't bother him. The trouble is I really love that apartment.

Then I think of Jamie. What about his school?

As if reading my mind, Helen laughs.

'Beth, the school I told you about in London, they still have a few places,. Call them. You never know Jamie might like it.'

Mum comes over and looks at me excitedly. 'Now tell me what's happening? Is it the apartment you like, the one near where we used to live?'

'Yes, Mum, it's in a mansion block, just off Queensway, close to the station. It needs a bit of work, but I can do that. It's on the first floor, facing the street. There's a small balcony which is amazing for London. The rooms are quite small but who cares and there's plenty of room for you.'

Jamie comes into the kitchen looking confused, probably wondering why everyone looks so happy. I just hope we can get him into the school.

'Is there any Cava in the fridge, Mum? I think this calls for a celebration, don't you?'

As we clink glasses, I think of Nick, I'll give DCI Thomas a call in the morning, tell him I'm moving to London.

35

LONDON
A few weeks later...

It's Friday and for a change I'm alone in the apartment. Mum's gone to Oxford to see one of her friends, she usually does this on a Friday, and Jamie's at school.

I stretch and pour myself another cup of coffee. Now what shall I do? Get started on my latest article for work, relax and watch TV, or go to the park for a walk?

This is one of the benefits of working freelance. The disadvantages are you don't get paid when you're sick and you don't get paid holidays.

The intercom phone buzzes.

It's Joe, the porter calling from downstairs.

'Hi Joe, what is it?'

'Beth, a hand delivered letter has been left for you, it's marked urgent.'

'I'll be down in a minute, thanks.'

Our apartments on the first floor so it's always quicker to take the stairs.

Two minutes later I'm in reception.

Joe greets me with a smile. 'Sorry, I didn't see who it was, I was on the phone, when I turned around it was on the desk.'

'Thanks Joe.'

On the front of the envelope is my name in large black, block capital letters - BETH - very strange, the writing doesn't look familiar. I turn to go upstairs but the woman who lives above me comes over.

'I'm sorry to interrupt. I just overheard what you said. I wasn't intentionally listening to you, I don't want to appear like a busybody, it's just that - well, I saw him, the person who delivered the letter.'

I don't usually receive letters by hand, so I'm interested to see what she has to say. 'Great, what did he or she look like?'

She laughs. 'He was wearing a long black coat and one of those Russian style hats.'

'Did you see his face?' I ask, hopefully.

She stands frowning, then shakes her head. 'It was so quick, he just popped the envelope on the desk, then walked out. I think he had a beard, but I'm not sure, it could have been a scarf.'

I thank her and run upstairs to our apartment and rip it open. A piece of paper falls onto the floor.

COME TO HOLLAND PARK MAIN ENTRANCE 9.00PM TONIGHT - DON'T TELL THE POLICE.

For some reason, I've been expecting this. The other day

I was in a car park loading the car with groceries and I had a strange feeling I was being watched.

I drove home and watched in my rear mirror to see if I was being followed, but saw nothing unusual.

The next day,

when I was on the small kitchen balcony, I had the weirdest feeling I was being watched. I remember looking down, but there was nothing unusual. I get this feeling a lot, I think I'm being followed, I'm not imagining it. DCI Thomas told me to call him if I think something's wrong, but he's in Oxford.

The front door suddenly opens, it's Mum.

'I thought you went to Oxford, Mum. What happened?'

She flops down on the sofa. 'I did, but I didn't feel too good, so I took the next train back to London. I took the 36 bus from Paddington to Queensway, so much traffic, I should have walked.'

She gets up and goes to the kitchen. 'Would you like a cup of tea or coffee?' she calls.

'Nothing thanks.'

Mum looks pale, but she often does lately. If only she would stop running around. Mum and Dad are getting divorced, and this is how she deals with it. She still hasn't said much, but I can see she's stressed.

Suddenly she pops her head round the kitchen door. 'I'm alright Beth, don't worry, it must have been something I ate last night. I thought the pizza tasted funny.'

Shall I tell her? I don't want to worry her, but if I don't...

She comes in with her coffee and sits down.

'Mum, look at this.' I pass her the letter. 'It was hand delivered today.'

Her eyes widen as she reads the note. 'Did you phone DCI Thomas?'

'Not yet, I...'

'Call him, or I will.'

Of course, she's right.

I grab my phone and call him; it goes to voicemail. I leave a message saying it's urgent and to call me.

Within minutes, he's on the phone asking me to scan the letter over to him. He gives me strict instructions not to go outside and says he'll see me soon.

Mum's making cheese on toast. I sit watching the news.

Then I think about Nick— did he leave the note? I keep thinking of him sitting in the garden talking to me, how nice he was. I was really getting to like him.

'I'm going to the park for a walk, Mum, to get some fresh air. I'll be back in a minute.'

'You can't, you heard what DCI Thomas said,' she says, coming into the hall with her toast.

'Well, he's not here, is he?'

'But Beth...'

'Sorry Mum, but I have to go out for a bit to clear my head.'

She looks so worried, so I quickly add.

'I'll be careful. I'll just go for a walk up to the top of Queensway and back.'

36

LONDON
Holland Park

I DON'T TAKE LONG, it's too cold, just a brisk walk, then I'm back at home. Mums tidied up and coffee's bubbling away in the kitchen.

Not long after getting back my phone rings.

'Beth, just to let you know everything's been arranged for tonight, so don't worry, when you go to Holland Park, you'll be covered.'

'By covered, what do you mean?'

'You won't be in any danger, just act naturally, they mustn't know they're being watched.'

'Will you be with me?'

'Beth, this area is covered by the Metropolitan police. A very good friend of mine called Inspector Hawes will contact you soon. Just do what he says, he'll call you before you leave and go over it with you. Now take down his number just in case you need to call him.'

The next few hours pass very slowly. Jamie comes home from school; Mum and I try to act as if nothing's wrong and make dinner. Mum's worried something will go wrong and who can blame her. My insides are churning, I feel sick, so I make mint tea which helps a bit.

At 8.10 pm, there's a call from Inspector Hawes.

'Hello Beth, I know DCI Thomas spoke to you earlier, I'm just following up to introduce myself and make sure you're OK. If you have any worries don't hesitate to call me, you have my number?'

'Yes.'

'In fifteen minutes go and collect your car and drive to the park. We will be in contact with you all the time so don't be worried. Just drive to the spot indicated in the letter and wait.'

When the time comes I walk round to where the car park is. It's quiet now. If it wasn't for the lights in the overhead apartments it would be pitch black and creepy.

Holland Park's not far away so it doesn't take long to drive there. When I near the main entrance I slow down and park near a streetlight. I can't see anyone outside, but they're hardly going to make themselves conspicuous are they?

Twenty minutes later I'm still waiting, nobody's shown up. Maybe it's a prank. I'm sat here like an idiot, no phone calls, no tap on the car window, nothing. I look around, deciding what to do next, then call DCI Thomas.

'It's me, what's happening?'

'I know as much as you do, Beth.'

He sounds slightly irritated probably because he's not in charge.

'I can't just sit here; shall I get out and stand in front of the entrance so they can see me?'

He pauses for a moment. 'I'll call you back in a minute.'

A minute passes, then my phone rings, it's DCI Thomas.

'Okay, stand in front of the entrance, we've got you covered.'

I'm walking up and down, then I look around expecting to see Nick, hiding behind a tree.

Where the hell is he?

Hardly anyone's around, just me and a few people coming home from work or a night out.

My phone rings. It's DCI Thomas.

'Beth, get in your car, drive home, and we'll see if anyone follows you.'

The drive back is uneventful, I park in the street outside our apartment, not in the car park, it's dark around the back and too damn creepy, just the sort of place someone would jump you.

Mums in the kitchen looking worried. 'What happened, Beth?'

I shrug. 'A waste of time, nobody showed up.'

'Where've you been Mum,' Jamie asks, coming into the kitchen. 'I didn't know you went out?'

I left him watching *The Philosopher's Stone,* his favourite Harry Potter film.

'Oh, I just popped out for some milk, did you enjoy the film?'

'Yeah, it was great. Can I have a hot chocolate?'

'Of course, but first I must make a call, be back in a minute.'

I close my bedroom door and call DCI Thomas; he picks up immediately.

'I don't know what happened tonight, Beth. We're checking to see if there's anything suspicious, we're going through the CCTV outside the park, maybe we missed something. I'll call you tomorrow, and don't go out, okay?'

It reminds me of when I was a virtual prisoner in Oxford — the police outside — Nick always being so concerned, making me stay at home when he knew damn well...

'Beth, are you still there?' he snaps.

'Yes, I was just thinking about Nick and the sighting of him in the Lake District. Have you heard anymore?'

He says nothing. Is there something he's not telling me?

'Oh, I thought I told you. It turns out it wasn't him, just someone who looks like him. We heard something about him being seen in Spain, but I'm still waiting for more details.'

'But Nick's not stupid. He knows how the police work. He's probably lying low for a while until this quietens down. If he's in Spain, he's not coming back here knowing the police are after him.'

He grunts. 'I know that's what I thought. Anyway, forensics has the letter you gave me. We may have some news tomorrow. Now go to bed, try to sleep.'

Jamie's in bed, Mum's drinking wine and watching a late-night film.

'I'm going to make a tea, Mum. Do you want anything?'

'No thanks. Jamie went to bed; I think he's doing some homework.'

I raise my eyebrows. 'Very good. Did he have his hot chocolate?'

'Yes, I made it.'

I go into the kitchen. It's strange, but even in here I feel I'm being watched; psychiatrists would probably say it's because of what happened, but I still get the feeling I'm being followed.

While I wait for the kettle to boil, I glance out of the window. It's windy and getting much colder now. Summer's gone, and the long winter nights are drawing in.

I take my tea out onto the small kitchen balcony. A few people pass by. They all look so normal, but what did I expect? Someone standing under a streetlight, reading a newspaper. His collar turned up, his hat pulled down.

I stand sipping my tea, surveying the street then freeze. A glint of light from a car below catches my eye. Is someone inside the car smoking?

Ten minutes later I'm still watching the car, hands cupping my mug of tea to keep warm. After a couple of minutes, I go inside.

Mum looks up as I go into the living room. 'Is everything alright?' she says, giving me a worried look. 'What did DCI Thomas say?'

'He said he'll get back to me in the morning.'

She says nothing, just frowns. 'Well, they'd better do something soon. Did he say anything about Nick? Have they found him?'

'He said there's been a sighting of him in Spain. Don't worry Mum, they'll get him soon.'

She puts down her empty glass of wine and looks at me. 'But I am worried Beth, if he's in Spain, who sent you that letter?'

37

Later that night...

What was that?

I sit listening. All I can hear is my heartbeat.

I'm sure I heard something.

Maybe it was a cat outside, or people coming home from a night out? Whatever it was, it woke me.

I wish I had my Glock — I feel so vulnerable.

Shall I get a knife? What time is it?

My phones under my pillow. I drag it out and peak at it — 3.20 in the morning. I must go back to sleep. DCI Thomas is calling me tomorrow, and he gets up early.

I close my eyes, then freeze. It's as if Mum's cat, Tabitha, jumped on my bed. But Tabitha's in Oxford. She's staying with Mum's next-door neighbour.

I turn over to reach for the light switch.

What the fuck!

Something's over my mouth, I can't shout, I can't move, it's that same smell, then everything goes hazy.

I CAN HEAR my phone ringing, then it stops. I try to sit up, but my head feels heavy. Then I remember — someone was in my room.

I half crawl out of bed. Everything's blurred. I look down — my nighty, my pants, where are they?

What happened?

I stand, holding my head, looking around the room. It all looks the same. I grab my dressing gown, my phone rings. It's DCI Thomas. I stand staring at the phone. I can't move, I feel heavy.

Mum knocks. I can't move. She knocks again, then opens the door.

'Didn't you hear your phone? DCI Thomas just phoned me; he wants to talk to you.' Then she stops. 'Beth! What's wrong? You look as if you've seen a ghost?'

She leads me over to my bed; I sit down and tell her what happened. She grabs my phone; presses redial, DCI Thomas answers.

I sit listening to her talking — my head's fuzzy. I don't know what happened.

I go to the bathroom, lock the door and look at myself. No bruises, no cuts, I'm not in pain. I sit on the toilet seat, hands over my face. I want to remember, but I can't.

The next few hours are a blur. DCI Thomas suggests I have some tests taken, just to be sure I'm OK. He drops us off then goes back to the station.

After they've done all the tests, Mum gets me a cup of tea, then we sit and wait for the results.

Much later, maybe an hour, but it could be less, a policewoman comes in.

'Sorry, for the long wait.' She hesitates and looks at me, and I know by her expression what's coming. I shake my head. *No! Please tell me it's not what I'm thinking.*

'It's not good, not what we hoped for.' She puts her hand on my arm. 'I know this is difficult. The forensics team is at your house right now.'

What happened in Oxford was bad enough, but this! I sit staring ahead. I want to shout — I want to scream. I want to kill whoever did this.

How did they get in? Did I leave the kitchen balcony door open? I'm sure I locked it; I always do.

'I can arrange for a car to take you home if you like,' murmurs the policewoman.

I hear Mum say no, we'll get a taxi.

The taxi pulls up outside our block. The police are just leaving. Mum stops and talks to them. I rush inside straight to the kitchen. I want to see if they've tampered with the balcony door.

Mum comes running in after me. 'Sit in the living room, Beth. I'll make us a coffee, or would you rather have a brandy?'

I swing round and look at her. 'The door lock, it's broken. How could they do this without us hearing?'

She sighs. 'Whoever it was knew what they were doing. Forensics have checked everything.' She fills two glasses with brandy and hands me one. I gulp it down and lie on the sofa. She sits on a chair near the window drinking her brandy.

———

THE NEXT THING I know the phone's ringing.

I'm still on the sofa. Mum must have covered me — the small lamp is on. How long have I slept?

Mum comes into the room. 'Beth, it's DCI Thomas. Do you want to talk to him?'

I shake my head. 'What time is it?'

'It's just gone 6.00 in the evening. Are you sure? He might have some news.'

I shake my head; she closes the door.

I don't want to think about it. Pulling the cover up over my head, I close my eyes and try to sleep, but all I can see is Nick.

Did he do this?

38

Much later that evening...

I CAN HEAR Jamie whispering to Mum, it's 10.45 in the evening. I'll freshen myself up then see them.

Jamie looks up when I walk into the kitchen. Mum quickly pulls out a chair and gives me a wink.

'How do you feel? You won't be eating any more of those pizzas, will you?'

Jamie's watching me strangely. I can tell he doesn't believe Mum.

Mum fills a bowl with soup and places it in front of me.

'She'll be alright, don't worry Jamie, this soup will make your mum feel better.'

Jamie comes and sits beside me.

'Anything I can do, Mum?'

I ruffle his hair and kiss him. 'I just need to get this bowl of soup down me, then I'll be as right as rain.'

He keeps looking at me, a worried look on his face. I hug him to me. 'No more pizzas for me for a while.'

It's late, so after I eat, he reluctantly goes to sleep. An hour later, so does Mum. I stay in the living room, I can't go near my bedroom.

———

EARLY NEXT MORNING I'm in the kitchen making coffee when my phone rings. It's DCI Thomas.

'Sorry, I couldn't talk yesterday. I hope you understand.'

'Of course, I'm sorry this happened, Beth. I just want you to know...'

He stops for a few seconds; I can hear him breathing.

'You know who it was, don't you?'

'No, Beth, but I think I know where Nick is.'

I hold my breath and wait.

'Don't get your hopes up, these sightings can be misleading, but from what I know, he was last seen heading for the port in Malaga. He's probably trying to get a boat. The Spanish police are onto it. I'll let you know as soon as I hear anything.'

So, who was it?

As if reading my mind, he blurts out. 'If he's in Spain, then you know what that means.' He stops, then quickly adds. 'We've got all the ports and airports covered, so...'

I really thought it was Nick, but why would he come here? If he's on the run, and after all that's happened, I hardly think he'd be visiting me.

'Then who was it?'

'We don't know, Beth. It'll take time to find out. It could've been a random act, but we'll soon find out, I promise you. I'll be in touch as soon as I know something, in the meantime, think seriously about taking that trip to Athens.'

I can't believe he just said that. It's the same old thing they all keep saying - get out of the country, forget about it, but it won't help, it will never stop until I find out who did it.

I stand staring down at the street below. *If it wasn't Nick, who was it? Major Oliver Hudson and the rest of those evil people are in prison, aren't they?*

The kitchen phone suddenly rings. It's DCI Thomas again.

'Beth, I'm sorry to trouble you again, but there's been a fresh development.'

From the sound of his voice, I know it's something awful. 'Yes, what is it?'

'I'll come to that in a minute, but first let me run through some things with you. You were right about Nick. He was on drugs, probably still is, but there's something else. 'It's about the Major.'

I feel sick. 'But he's in prison.'

'Yes, he is, Beth. But the Major has his finger in many pies. He befriends people, gets them used to the good life, if you can call it that, and then he gets them hooked on drugs. The rest is easy. Anyway, Nick wasn't the only one. We're investigating the Detective Superintendent, seems he also dabbles in drugs.'

'So, what are you saying?'

'Well, from what we've discovered, he's been doing this for years. We've also contacted Interpol...'

'You think the Major had something to do with this?'

'Beth, the Major's a very dangerous man with many friends in high places. I thought you should know, you must be vigilant. Don't go out alone.'

'But you must do something! What do other people do

in my situation? In films, they get a new identity, live in a different country, but I can't do that. Where would I get the money from, for starters?' A cold rush of anger sweeps over me. *I won't let them terrorise me like this.*

'Look, I know this is hard,' he says, in a worried sounding voice. 'But believe me, we are dealing with it. We have the best criminal minds working on this case. The net's tightening, people are squealing, they're hoping to get a shorter sentence. Many influential heads are going to fall, but until that happens, we must look after you and your family.'

I sit listening, not really taking in what he's saying. All I want is to find whoever did this to me. I want to...

'Beth, are you listening?'

'Yes.'

'Now listen, carefully, this is what you must do. I've arranged flights for you and they leave tomorrow.'

'What!'

'Yes, this is serious, Beth. We're getting you out of here for a while. Your mother knows she's going with you, and of course Jamie. She's packed a few things. The police collected them. She'll take the train as usual in the morning to Oxford. Jamie's going with her. She's told him not to say anything, it's a surprise — you're all going to Athens for a brief holiday.'

I can't believe what I'm hearing.

'I'll come to your place, all very normal. We'll get you out the back way. Helen knows about it; you'll be staying with her.'

'I don't have much choice, do I?'

'It's the best we could do at such short notice, Beth.'

NEXT DAY

Mum and Jamie are on their way to Oxford. Mum tells me not to worry. The police will follow them to make sure nothing goes wrong. They'll go to her place, have lunch, then take a cab to Heathrow Airport.

A couple of hours later, DCI Thomas arrives at my apartment. I make sure everything's locked up, then take the back way out of the block where a car is waiting to drive me to Heathrow Airport.

It doesn't take long as there's not much traffic.

Twenty-five minutes later and I'm at the airport. Mum and Jamie are having drinks in a private waiting room. Of course, Jamie's over the moon and finds it all very exciting - he thinks Mum arranged it.

The plane takes off at 5.10 pm, so 7.00 in the evening Athens time.

We settle down for the flight to Athens. I haven't eaten all day; I've lost my appetite. All I want is for this to be over, for things to be normal again.

I look over at Jamie, tucking into his sandwich, and vow to get whoever did this to us.

It's late when we arrive — just gone 11.00 at night. DCI Thomas arranged for us to be taken through customs and led out through a special exit, just to be on the safe side, and Helen's there to meet us.

'Beth!'

She comes running over to us, hugs me, then Jamie and Mum.

'How lovely to see you all!'

Jamie's eyes are huge with excitement. He can't get over the intrigue of it all.

Helen grabs his hand. 'Come with me. The car's parked right outside, so we don't have far to walk.'

As we drive along I inhale the scent of the sea, the warmth of the evening and the scent of jasmine.

When we reach Helen's house, we find all the beds freshly made and ready to climb into. Jamie's too tired to eat anything, and so is Mum who soon retires to bed.

Helen and I sit on the balcony talking long into the early hours of the morning.

39

HELEN'S HOUSE

ATHENS
7.30 am

We've been here for two days, the weather's lovely, still a healthy 25 degrees, and so far, we're safe.

DCI Thomas calls me daily, still no news about Nick, but there's lots of news from London about my case. People are being arrested, including many in high places, but the person who raped me is still on the loose.

Jamie's school is under the impression one of his close Greek relatives is getting married, what else could I tell them. Fortunately, the head was nice about it.

It's just gone 7.30 in the morning. Mum and Jamie are still in bed, Helen's gone to work, she starts early, most people in Athens do during the long hot summer months.

I take my coffee onto the balcony so I can enjoy the fresh morning air. After my second sip my phone rings. It's DCI Thomas.

'Good morning, Beth, how are things in Athens?'

He's up early, he sounds happier than usual; I hear the rustle of papers, then he's back on the phone.

'I'm going to tell you something highly confidential, it's about an arrest the police have made regarding your case.'

My heart skips a beat. *Will this nightmare soon be over?*

'The Major paid someone to... to do this to you.' He pauses for a few seconds, then carries on. 'He used to work for him, at the farm.'

I'm holding the phone very tightly.

They've caught him, they've actually caught him!

I open my mouth to say something, but the words don't come out.

'Did you hear me, Beth?'

'Yes,' I mutter. 'Are you sure?'

'Of course. As I said before, people are squealing, it always happens. They're either looking for a way out, nobody wants to go to prison, or they've got revenge on their mind. This boy, or rather man, he's twenty-eight, has been spending a lot of money, which is unusual for him as he doesn't have much. He's been drinking and boasting about his latest conquest, describing what he did in graphic detail.'

I feel sick. I take a deep breath.

He carries on talking. 'We got a tip from his girlfriend. It seems a friend of hers heard him bragging about it in the pub, so she goes and calls her friend. Of course she's furious and calls the police.'

As I listen to him, I keep thinking I'm having a bad dream and that it will soon stop, but it doesn't.

'Are you still there, Beth?'

'Yes,' I croak.

'Shall I carry on?' he asks, in a worried voice. 'You know we can do this later.'

'No, tell me, I want to know.'

'Well, the following evening we had one of our undercover men in this pub. We had it all set up, and it worked. The guy was drinking heavily and blabbing as usual about his conquest. His girlfriend came in. She was furious, she had a go at him, he laughed in her face, he said...'

Then he stops talking.

'Beth, are you alright? I know this must be a shock, but we've got him. You can come home.'

I don't know whether to laugh or cry. It's just so awful. It's like it happened to someone else, but he's talking about me — it happened to me.

40

LONDON

I'M on my way to the café in the park. A few tourists and mothers with kids are sitting outside, but not so many as the last time I was here with Helen.

She popped over to see me the other weekend, which was nice. She still wants me to come back to Athens, but for now, I'm staying here.

Jamie's settling into school, which is a relief for both of us. He seems to enjoy living in London and has some friends. I still don't know where Nick is. DCI Thomas told me not to worry, the Spanish police think he boarded a ship in Malaga. They say he might have gone to Algeria or Morocco, but could still be in Spain. They'll update DCI Thomas if they find out where he is.

I take the coffee I just bought to one of the wooden benches and sit, thinking of Nick. If he's in Spain, why do I feel I'm being followed? I often think I'm going a little crazy, and what with all that's happened, I probably am. It's just that...

When I go shopping, or when I'm walking around Queensway late at night, I often get a whiff of Nick's cologne.

I haven't told Mum. I think she's had enough of London and is looking for somewhere to live in Greece, which means I'll either have to change jobs or get someone to live in to look after Jamie when I'm out on a job.

I told Helen, and she said it's my mind playing tricks on me, and that many men use this cologne. It's just that when I get a whiff, I automatically think of him. I know what she means, but I can't help feeling I'm still being followed.

41

LONDON
 Late evening...

He stares ahead at the woman slowly crossing the road, laden with heavy shopping.

Autumnal leaves coat the black, shiny street still wet from the rain. She's going to slip, he thinks, any minute now.

She crosses the street unscathed as he scratches his head. He looks in his rear-view mirror, checking to see if anyone else is wandering around a residential street at close to midnight.

He tries to get more comfortable, takes off his seatbelt and stares ahead. Physically drained, he rubs his eyes, then he's fully alert. Someone switched on a light at number 8.

He watches as the woman dumps the heavy shopping on the counter, then she disappears away from view for a while.

Ten minutes later, she returns to the kitchen, switches on the kettle, then takes a couple of mugs out of a cupboard.

A younger woman joins her in the kitchen. They're chatting and laughing about something. He cracks his knuckles and looks in the rear-view mirror again. It's such a quiet street, and he's now very aware of the sound of his watch ticking.

He looks up and sees that the younger woman is alone in the kitchen. He concentrates on her as she spoons coffee into the mugs. A boy calls her from another room. She quickly scoops up the mugs, the lights go off, and she's gone.

It's rather late for the boy to still be up, and on a school night too. Soon, someone will switch on the bedroom light and turn it off around an hour later.

He knows her routine now. He also knows when she's alone.

THE END

Beth returns in Book 2 - The Killing

Buy on Amazon ~ FREE in Kindle Unlimited!

JUST A FEW WORDS...

If you enjoyed *Followed* it would be great if you could leave a review on Amazon. Just a few words makes a huge difference.

Cara

BOOK 2 - FIRST CHAPTER
SHE'S A JOURNALIST…SHE'S NO STRANGER TO THE DARKER SIDE OF LIFE…

Athens, 4 February, 10.15pm in the evening...

'We need to meet, all I want is a few minutes of your time.'

James grunts. He has no idea who the man is or why he's calling him, and he's getting pissed off.

'You won't tell me your name, so why should I bother?'

'It's urgent,' the rasping Greek voice hisses. 'It's a matter of life and death. You can stop someone from being killed, you must come!' He lowers his voice, just a little. 'Do you know Fanis Bar, in Glyfada? It's off the main highway, the bar with the terrace outside?'

James starts to say something, but the Greek carries on.

'I'll be there at 10.30, be there.'

Then he hangs up.

James stands staring at his phone. *Is the guy mad or just winding me up?*

Gulping down the rest of the coffee he's just bought from the cafe across the square, he crumples the now empty polystyrene cup into a ball, tosses it into a nearby bin, then crosses the road to a small side street where his car's parked.

All he wants is to go home, have a beer, put his feet up, but he can't, he's arranged to meet Helen. She said it was urgent so he can't let her down.

He clicks his key fob, the car springs into action.

His phone rings - number withheld.

James stares at his phone.

Is it that crazy Greek again?

'Yes,' he snaps.

'I want you to understand how important this is, it is of international concern, this man's life is in danger, we must do something to stop it.'

Oh my God, the guy just doesn't give up, but for some strange reason James has a gut feeling about this. It could be the scoop of a lifetime, he might be wrong, but what if the guy is telling the truth?

'Okay, but it'd better be good, what do you look like?'

The man sighs with relief. 'I'm wearing a brown velvet jacket and a striped scarf.'

'I'll be there in about fifteen minutes,' James mutters.

He slides into his car, switches on the air con and calls Helen to say he'll be a little late.

She sounds irritated but agrees to wait for him, she

knows if he has a bee in his bonnet about a story there's no stopping him.

Ten minutes later he's out of the center of Athens heading towards the upmarket beachside resort of Glyfada.

As usual Posseidonas Avenue is busy, it's the main coastal road leading to other popular beachside resorts and also leads to Cape Sounion and the ruins of the Temple of Poseidon.

The neon lights of the restaurants and hotels shed a rainbow of colours over the highway that remind him of when he worked in London, clandestine meetings like this are now a thing of the past. He smiles to himself, that's probably why he agreed to see the guy.

Putting his foot down hard on the accelerator he urges his old car to go faster. Before moving to Athens he'd worked as a journalist but when his friend Beth invited him to her wedding in Athens, his whole life changed.

Within a matter of weeks, he'd handed in his notice, packed up his stuff in London, moved to Athens, and started a part time job at a local college teaching English. Thanks to an uncle's inheritance, he now owns a small delicatessen in Athens, and works part time as a journalist.

He starts to slow down; he doesn't want to miss the turning, it's around here somewhere. Drivers honk their horns in frustration as he edges the car over to the inside lane.

On leaving the highway he turns left into a tree lined street leading to *Fanis Bar*. Out of the corner of his eye he can see the guy, it must be him, he's the only one on the terrace. He's sitting with his legs crossed on an old rickety looking chair, nonchalantly smoking a cigarette.

James sits for a few seconds watching him. The guy's probably in his 40s or 50s, with longish brown hair and a thin moustache. There's a small glass of something in front of him which he picks up and slowly drinks, then he puts the glass down and draws deeply on his cigarette. He does this a few times, then looks around, probably wondering where James is.

Without bothering to lock the car door, James walks quickly up the couple of steps to the open bar terrace.

The man sees him, waves his hand and beckons him over. His dark eyes rest on James's face for a second, then he looks away. 'What will you drink?' he asks, flicking the ash off of his cigarette into the ashtray.

James pulls out another rickety looking chair opposite the Greek. 'A beer, thanks.'

The waiter leans against the open bar door smoking a cigarette, watching them. The Greek glances over to him and points to James.

'*Mia bira parakalo.*'

The waiter nods, takes another drag of his cigarette, flicks it into the night air and saunters inside the bar.

James leans back in his chair and studies the man opposite him. The Greek returns his gaze.

'So, what do you want to tell me?' James asks.

The Greek leans forward, slightly. 'I have some news that will shock you.' He stops for a minute, glances around at the nearby tables, then as if satisfied, carries on talking. 'You must not tell anyone what I'm about to tell you, if you do, your life and mine will be in danger.'

James nods.

'I can't tell you everything tonight. We will meet in a few days, in another place, and then I will tell you more. We must be careful, you understand?'

James raises an eyebrow, it all sounds a bit dramatic but hey, this is the land where Greek drama flourished in the late sixth century BC. He sits watching the Greek trying to fathom him out, he looks like an actor or he could be a teacher.

The man sits holding his gaze, his dark eyes defiant.

Suddenly James smiles. 'Don't worry, you can trust me.'

The man draws hard on his cigarette, blows a circle of smoke into the night air and leans closer to James. 'I have this on very good authority, they intend to kidnap the Prime Minister and kill him.' He looks at James intently, as if waiting for a reaction. James says nothing, so the Greek carries on. 'At the moment he's popular with some Greeks, but many want him out of the way.'

James sits looking at him wondering if the guy's for real, or just some crazy academic who's finally cracked. He could well understand this happening, they say the economy is recovering but many Greeks are still suffering. Thousands have left the country and those that remain are either very rich or struggling to make ends meet.

He sits watching the man opposite him with interest, just like many Greeks he smokes too much and always seems to be thinking. James shifts in his chair and scratches his head. If it's true what he says then he needs to know more, much more. Maybe his friend Dev is the person the man should be speaking to? This is his line of work; he has the necessary contacts.

James frowns. 'I'll have to discuss this with one of my colleagues, he has experience in this sort of thing. I also need to know who is behind this, when it's going to happen and where?'

The Greek's eyes narrow. 'How do I know I can trust your friend? What is his name?'

James looks at him in surprise, does the guy really expect him to tell him?

'If he agrees to help then I'll tell you his name, but don't worry, he's one of the best.' As an afterthought he adds. 'You haven't told me your name?'

The man's silent then waves his hand in the air dismissively, the way Greeks do, he lights another cigarette, his eyes never leave James's face.

'My name doesn't matter.'

James leans back in his chair and stares at him. 'Why all the secrecy, who are you?'

'As I said, my name doesn't matter, I prefer it this way.'

James shifts in his chair, the guy's beginning to irritate him. 'What about my phone number? How did you get that?'

The Greek smiles, slightly. 'It was easy. I went to your food shop. I told the Spanish woman working there I was an old friend of yours, that I needed to speak to you, I said it was very urgent and she told me.'

James's wife Isabelle often works in the delicatessen when it's busy, or when he's out. He's lost count of the times he's asked her not to give anyone his number.

Running his hand through his hair he surveys the man opposite him. 'It doesn't make sense, why choose me when there are so many Greek journalists who would jump at a scoop like this?'

The Greek shrugs his shoulders and looks at him. 'I read your newspaper articles, I know how you think, I've checked you out.' Then as an afterthought he adds. 'I have to be careful.'

The waiter saunters over, flicks the table with a red cloth, places a glass of beer in front of James, then walks back to the open bar door and lights a cigarette.

James sips the ice-cold beer relishing the moorish taste of the amber liquid. He sits watching the Greek for a few minutes, in a way he's enjoying the drama of the situation, he just wishes his friend Dev was here, he'd know what to do.

In his shirt pocket is a hundred-euro bill he keeps for occasions like this. He reaches inside his pocket, then stops. *Maybe the Greek will want more?*

As if reading his mind, the Greek waves his hand. 'I don't want your money, I just want you to take this seriously, they must be stopped.'

James nods, drains his beer and glances at his phone. It's getting late, he must hurry, Helen will be waiting for him.

He leans forward and picks up his car keys. 'When do you think this will happen?'

The man looks surprised. 'If I knew I would tell you, but it won't be long, I might find out more tonight, but you must promise not to repeat what I have said, otherwise...'

He makes a gesture across his neck.

'Don't worry, this is between you and me, I'll wait for your call.'

The man nods.

James stands up to go.

There's the sound of shooting - everything goes black for James.

The headlines on the Athens tabloid press the following morning read:

SHOOTING IN ATHENS BEACH BAR LATE THIS
EVENING - ONE DEAD, ONE ON LIFE SUPPORT
IN HOSPITAL

Buy on Amazon -- FREE in Kindle Unlimited!

A fast-paced crime thriller, *THE KILLING* is Book 2 in the exciting Beth Papadakis series.

BOOK 3 - PANIC
A SUICIDE BOMB ATTACK ON THE LONDON TUBE, A RUTHLESS HUMAN TRAFFICKING RING IN SPAIN...

This is the backdrop of Book 3 in the Beth Papadakis crime thriller series.

The chance of a job with the secret service puts Beth's life in turmoil. She's a journalist, but she needs a change. The job sounds tempting and it would mean working with Dev who works for MI6.

Desperate to make the right decision she heads for the warmer shores of Spain's Costa Tropical and her friend's hotel, she needs to rest, she needs to get her head together.

But what starts out as an idyllic vacation descends into chaos when she comes face to face with her nemesis and all hell breaks loose.

Buy on Amazon ~ FREE in Kindle Unlimited!

Set in the vibrant city of London, Spain's Costa Tropical, Costa del Sol and the old Moorish city of Granada.

BOOK 4 - PAYBACK
A GRIPPING FAST-PACED CRIME THRILLER...

Beth doesn't go looking for trouble, but trouble always seems to find her...

She's no stranger to the seedier side of life but this time she's stretched to the limit both emotionally and physically.

In one hell of a journey through Granada and southern Spain, Beth's confronted by ruthless drug and people traffickers.

As her every move is watched, she travels to the drug capital of Spain to rescue friends from a vicious kingpin of the drug and sex trade.

Buy on Amazon ~ FREE in Kindle Unlimited!

PAYBACK is a fast-paced edge of your seat thriller set in stunning locations.

BOOK 5 - PURE EVIL
AN EDGE OF YOUR SEAT THRILLER SET IN LONDON...

This dark, fast-paced crime thriller involves corruption in high places and draws you into the ruthless underbelly of organized crime in London's Mayfair.

Beth's back at work, but she's reporting on crime, not politics. Her new boss says he'll ease her in gently, but that's not what happens.

Still struggling emotionally and physically from the recent events in Spain, Beth's thrown in at the deep end. First there's the body of a young woman in Hyde Park, then a shooting takes place outside a casino in London's Mayfair.

Beth's sent to cover the Mayfair shooting of a popular croupier who, it seems, was involved with an MP. Her boss wants results, and he wants them now! Who murdered the two young women who met their untimely deaths in London's Mayfair?

Now it's up to Beth to deliver, and she does. She get's right into the hornet's nest and the organized crime scene in London, but what she discovers is so terrible - even worse, her life's now in danger.

PURE EVIL **is Book 5 in the exciting Beth Papadakis crime thriller series.**

Buy it on Amazon ~ FREE in Kindle Unlimited!

BOOK 6 - FALLOUT
AN EXCITING EDGE OF YOUR SEAT THRILLER...

Beth's back in another fast-paced thriller based in London...

She's asked to cover a terrorist attack with her colleague but things go terribly wrong in more ways than one...

Was it an inside job? Is there a mole in Westminster?

Then a detective's found dead.

Did he have links to organized crime? And why doesn't her boss let her cover this story?

While all this is happening Dev drops a bombshell which puts her life in turmoil.

Buy on Amazon FREE in Kindle Unlimited!

A crime thriller based in London, *FALLOUT* is Book 6 in the exciting Beth Papadakis series.

BOOK 7 - FATAL INTENT
BETH'S BACK ON THE CRIME BEAT IN THIS DARK, FAST-PACED CRIME THRILLER.

She's sent to cover a potential serial killer case in north London. Two women murdered already - is there going to be a third?

Her colleague Fred's sent to cover a hotel killing in London's Piccadilly, which could be disastrous for him.

In the meantime, Dev, who works for MI6, is being transferred to the Middle East.

He asked Beth to go with him - he's still waiting for an answer - how long will he wait?

Buy now on Amazon FREE in Kindle Unlimited

A crime thriller based in London, *FATAL INTENT* is Book 7 in the exciting Beth Papadakis series.

BOOK 8 - NEMESIS

Beth's back on the crime beat in London when she gets an urgent message to go to Athens... but a big story's about to break in the UK and her boss wants results today, not tomorrow...

This could be the scoop of the year for him, and he wants his best investigative reporters covering it - which means Beth and Fred.

She's had a lot of experience with drug and people trafficking in Spain, and Fred's a genius at hacking into computers...

Beth has no choice but to take the next flight to Athens, but what she discovers when she gets there is so terrible...

She's now in the dark underbelly of organized crime in Athens, hunting for a killer.

Can her colleague Fred cover for her while she's in Athens.

Buy on Amazon FREE in Kindle Unlimited!

NEMESIS is Book 8 in the dark, fast-paced Beth Papadakis crime thriller series.

BOOK 9 - IN TOO DEEP
A BETH PAPADAKIS LONDON CRIME REPORTER THRILLER

Beth and colleague Fred are covering a story of a dead body at Billingsgate Fish Market close to Canary Wharf, a top financial hub of the city of London. Then they're taken off the story — no reason given. They're then sent to cover a story that hit the news a few days ago at one of London's Tube stations — one that involves the wife of a top minister in government.

But unbeknown to their editor, Beth and Fred are still investigating the fish market murder. Is their editor up to his old tricks again? He always boasts of having friends in high places but has he gone too far this time? While all this is going on, Dev, who works for MI6, is on a very dangerous mission, but is this mission impossible?

IN TOO DEEP **is Book 9 in the exciting Beth Papadakis London crime reporter thriller series.**

Buy Now ~ Free on Kindle Unlimited!

BETH PAPADAKIS BOXSET : BOOKS 1 - 3
FOLLOWED : THE KILLING : PANIC

FOLLOWED

A gripping fast paced thriller that will keep you on the edge of your seat.

Beth's hopes of starting a new life in London come crashing down when she's attacked. She fights him off, but that's not the end of it...she's being followed.

Is there a stalker in the small village where this happened?

Unfortunately for Beth she soon discovers the depths of depravity some people will go to and the corruption that festers in the small village in the Cotswolds.

Her mum's on holiday in Spain, her young son hates his new school—she's at her wit's end to know what to do.

Then an old school friend who lives in the village where she was attacked surprises her by offering to help.

But is he trying to help, or does he have an ulterior motive?

The Killing

A fast-paced political suspense thriller full of twists and turns.

For the past few years Beth's been living in London, but a working trip to Athens takes an unexpected turn when disaster hits. Her friend Helen's life is in danger, and someone Beth meets has a lasting effect on her.

What starts as a day having lunch in an Athens casino, turns into something more sinister. A friend gets involved with the wrong people which could be fatal for him and Helen.

This is just the beginning of a dangerous journey that takes Beth from London to Athens and back again, into a world of violence, ruthlessness and revenge.

PANIC

A gripping fast-paced edge of your seat exciting suspense thriller.

The chance of a job with the secret service puts Beth's life in turmoil. She's a journalist but the job sounds really tempting.

Desperate to make the right decision, she heads for the warmer shores of Spain's Costa Tropical and her friend's hotel.

But what starts out as an idyllic vacation descends into chaos when she comes face to face with her nemesis.

Buy on Amazon FREE in Kindle Unlimited!

FREE BOOK

As I open the door, I hear someone behind me. Turning to see who it is, a fist smashes into my face, then another - I try pushing him away, but the punches keep coming. *I'm on the ground. I must get up - I must..*

Beth's a reporter, and when she gets news of what's happened to her friend, she jumps into her car. After going through a couple of red lights; she arrives at the hospital.

Still struggling emotionally with something similar that happened to her, she's stunned when she sees the terrible state her friend is in. Will she ever recover?

Now her reporter instincts kick in - there are no witnesses to the attack, no CCTV around the street where it happened. Is she prepared to risk everything to find the person who did this... she has a son to think of...

While all this is happening Beth's husband, who's a high-flying lawyer, reacts with indifference. He says she should think of her son - stop thinking about her friend and see a psychiatrist.

But Beth's having none of it. How dare he say she should see a shrink when he's out every night? He says he's going to meetings, but is he?

From the moment she investigates this heinous crime, things go terribly wrong in more ways than one, and now her life's in danger.

Get a FREE copy of Break Up when you join my VIP Club.

Join today for free at www.caraaalexander.com

You will also receive my books before they're published when you join my **ARC review team** just email me and I'll add you to the list!

ABOUT THE AUTHOR

I write fast-paced edge of your seat thrillers which I hope you enjoy reading as much as I do writing them. At the moment, I live in London, but I love to travel.

You can visit my website at: **https://www.caraaalexander.com.**

And if you want to keep up to date with my latest books and comments just follow me on my FB author page at: **Facebook.com/caraalexanderauthor**

I look forward to seeing you on the inside…

All the best, CARA

For my Family with love

Printed in Great Britain
by Amazon